T0065532

ENDORSEMENTS

Jerry Bergman brings courage to all his writing. I've been a fan of his groundbreaking work for twenty years. So it didn't surprise me that he tackled what is considered the most difficult abortion circumstance, a child conceived in rape. Bravo Dr. Bergman!

Bob Enyart
Radio Talk Show Host and Director, American Right To Life

In crafting this novel, Dr. Jerry Bergman, a distinguished author of over four dozen scholarly works pertaining to science and history, has chosen to draw on his expertise in the fields of psychology, sociology, and criminal justice. Dr. Bergman brings his firsthand knowledge, as well as his writing mastery, to present a behind-the-scenes perspective that may very well challenge one's views on some controversial issues facing our society today. At the very least, this engaging narrative will grip the reader's emotions and hold their curiosity and attention to the very end.

In Part II, "Marrying Jezebel", Dr. Jerry Bergman's tells the story of a marriage gone very wrong. It is a down-to-earth tale of duty and deception, business and betrayal, infidelity and infatuation, matrimony and manipulation. Though focused on the teen and early adult years of protagonist Billy Kline, Bergman's characters span three generations and mention such topics as the Holocaust, hunting, high school, and Hollywood. If you enjoy stories where not everything is as it appears, plots that have twists and turns, narratives where the victimized is sometimes the villain, epics of love lost and love found, then this is your next good read.

David V. Bassett, M.S.

This story is written by an award-winning author with firsthand knowledge and experience in both corrections and psychology. As such, his knowledge is critical and compelling in helping the reader understand events behind this engaging story. The events move rapidly, providing the detail required to understand the characters and their social relevance, while not overwhelming the reader. The book is both educational and informative. It contains a clear scriptural message, and once I started, I was unable to put down this engrossing tale that addresses several of the most important social issues of our time.

Kevin H. Wirth
CEO Leafcutter Press

How
GREAT EVIL
Birthed
GREAT GOOD
Inspired by the True Story of Two Families

Jerry Bergman, Ph.D.

WESTBOW
PRESS®
A DIVISION OF THOMAS NELSON
& ZONDERVAN

This is a work of fiction. All of the characters, names, incidents, organizations, and dialogue in this novel are either the products of the author's imagination or are used fictitiously.

WestBow Press books may be ordered through booksellers or by contacting:

WestBow Press
A Division of Thomas Nelson & Zondervan
1663 Liberty Drive
Bloomington, IN 47403
www.westbowpress.com
844-714-3454

The Holy Bible, Berean Study Bible, BSB Copyright ©2016, 2018 by Bible Hub Used by Permission. All Rights Reserved Worldwide.

Scripture taken from the Amplified Bible, Copyright © 1954, 1958, 1962, 1964, 1965, 1987 by The Lockman Foundation. Used with permission.

ISBN: 978-1-6642-2019-5 (sc)
ISBN: 978-1-6642-2018-8 (hc)
ISBN: 978-1-6642-2020-1 (e)

Library of Congress Control Number: 2021901608

Print information available on the last page.

WestBow Press rev. date: 06/28/2021

DEDICATION

To my wife, Dianne, who has proven a homecoming queen can rear wonderful children and be a devoted wife and grandmother.

INTRODUCTION BY THE AUTHOR

I n my work in corrections in a prison, and as a therapist at Arlington Psychological Associates, I was privileged to work with a wide variety of clients. I also traded experiences with coworkers and others. One account I came across was the inspiration of this story. It struck me that it must be told because the story teaches very important lessons about forgiveness and both the good and evil side of humanity. Many details were changed to protect the privacy of the families involved, other details were embellished to allow the story to f low forward in a logical narrative.

ACKNOWLEDGEMENTS

I especially want to thank Marilyn Dauer, M.A., David V. Bassett, M.S., DeeDee Plettner, John Thomas, R.N., and my wife Dianne Haldiman Bergman for their help and encouragement during the crafting of this story. Most scripture quotations were from the Berean Study Bible, February 21, 2020 draft version which will be updated before the planned printing later in 2020. *The Holy Bible, Berean Study Bible*, BSB Copyright ©2016, 2018, 2019 by Bible Hub; used by permission. All rights reserved worldwide.

CONTENTS

PART 1

PART II

PART 1
Rebekah Martin's Story

CHAPTER 1
My Life Changes Forever

My name is Rebekah Marie Martin and this is my story. It was 10:30 at night and I had just put in a long day at the local hospital where I was a nurse. As I drove home, I was feeling good about my life, my career, my boyfriend, and the moonlit evening. The weather was perfect; not too hot or too cold. I pulled up into the parking lot next to my apartment, which was on the second floor of the old stately building in front of me. After I parked, I sat in my car for a few minutes to finish listening to one of my favorite songs then playing on the radio. As I opened the door and began to get out of my car, I saw a chrome plated hand gun by my car window held by a large Black man. He said in a commanding voice, "Get back in the car and keep your mouth shut if you don't want to get hurt."

I was stunned—terrified! This event turned out to be a nightmare, by far the worst day of my life! He forced me to lay down on the bench front seat of my car. I remember he still held the gun while he laid on top of me. I was afraid that the gun would go off accidentally or, worse, deliberately. I remembered part of my nursing training for this horror and tried to think of things I could do to help me survive this nightmare, praying it would end soon and I would still be alive. My arm was twisted and his weight hurt me. He was a big man. He must have been six feet or taller. I was a virgin and he was not gentle, seemingly wanting to hurt me. In pain much of the time, I clenched my fists and focused on this torment ending. It did eventually, but seemed like an eternity. In nursing school I learned rape is a crime of power, an attempt to hurt and humiliate. It sure was this in my case.

When it was finally over, he said, "Stay in the car until you see I'm gone. If you attempt to get out of the car, I'll kill you, so don't try anything foolish! Got it?" I sat there somewhat relieved as at least I had survived, so far. When I could no longer see him, I sat there for what seemed like fifteen minutes or longer. What should I do now?

I was bleeding, so I drove back to the hospital, directly to the emergency room. While driving, I realized I was disoriented even though I had driven this route many times. Somehow, I made it to the hospital. I told the nurse on duty, whom I did not recognize, what happened. She put me in a wheelchair and chauffeured me to the Forensics Center in the university-affiliated hospital where I worked.

When there, I told the doctor I was raped, was a virgin, and was now in severe pain and bleeding. He checked me over for bleeding, which had stopped then, thank goodness, and gave me some pain meds and sedatives to calm me down—Xanax, I think. When I was somewhat stabilized, the detective from the local police department, Officer Williams, came in and began asking me a series of questions about the rape.

"Could you describe him?"

"It was dark, so I cannot give you a very detailed description."

"I understand. Just tell me as much as you can remember," he added to encourage me to respond.

"He was about six feet tall, 180 pounds, maybe 200; had a dark complexion, kinky hair, and he had a slight skin problem."

"His eye color?"

"I don't remember. I was too frightened to notice. It was dark and I did not look into his eyes. Look, I was being raped!! Maybe they were dark brown. I'm guessing."

"Anything else? You have described about a third of the Black population. Any tattoos, scars, unusual mannerisms? Did he have a widow's peak? Was he losing his hair? Balding?"

"No. Look, I was terrified." My past experience ran by me like a movie then, just as I've heard from others who believed they were dying. I thought, "Would I ever see my special guy, my boyfriend, again?"

"Okay. I understand. Describe as best you can the events leading up to the rape, during, and after it."

"I will try, but the medication is kicking in now, so I may make some mistakes."

"I understand. I have done a lot of these investigations in my career, so I fully understand."

"Thank you." I answered, still shaking from the trauma of the evening.

"Anything unusual you saw? What about his voice? Was he a stutterer?"

"No, nothing unusual at all. He was an average, big, tall Black man."

"Did you know him? Have you ever seen him before?"

"No, I don't remember seeing him before. And I'm very good at remembering faces," I added.

Then Officer Williams remarked, "I will also record the weather for this evening on my report. The crime you experienced is rare on real cold days and blistery hot days, so with good weather like this we have more rapes. Okay, please tell me any other details of what happened."

I then told Officer Williams the details of the whole story, all that I could remember, that is.

He then said he would type up the police report, which I could review in a day or so.

"The main way we apprehend rapists is to develop place, time and modus operandi patterns, so all of this helps," Officer Williams said, as he flashed a warm smile, attempting to reassure me.

"Then we can work to determine if your rape matched others in the area, which helps us in our investigation. We usually find patterns that help us apprehend possible suspects," he added.

"I understand."

"Oh, one more thing. We will need to impound your car as, besides the rape kit, it is the key evidence in this case. We will check your car for fingerprints, hair evidence, and anything else that could help solve the case and apprehend the perpetrator. We will need a month or so to do the investigation. So we will have to impound your car until we finish the forensics work."

"A month? What will I do to get around until then?"

"This is standard procedure, ma'am. You should have called the police as soon as the offense occurred, and not drive the car, which contaminates the crime scene," he added.

"I'm sorry, this is the first time I've been raped. Actually the first time I have had sex with anybody, and I was bleeding quite profusely, so I felt I needed to get to the hospital as soon as possible."

"I understand. No problem. Could you tell me where the car is parked now, and the make and model of the vehicle?"

"It's parked in Lot D here at the hospital. My car is a red, 1974 Chevy Sedan, Texas license number KN 2274."

"OK. We will send a truck to get it and let you know when you can pick it up. It may be a while. Do you have the keys?"

"Yes." I then reached into my purse, looking for them. "Here they are," I announced, not too happy to lose my car for a month.

"Thank you for your cooperation. We need to catch this guy and lock him up as soon as possible. Most rapists are serial rapists—it's often a compulsion. They rape over and over. When we catch one, it usually clears lots of rape cases. So we need to catch this guy as soon as possible to stop him from doing it again."

"Yes, I agree," I added, now very tired from the medication. "Thank you for your help," he said before he left.

After the officer's departure, I then tried to call my boyfriend, Robert, but he didn't answer. I tried again a few minutes later and, yet again, no answer.

The doctor, Dr. Beltz, then walked in and took some blood and sent it to the lab for evaluations. Plus he did an examination for lacerations and other concerns. He also took vagina swabs as part of the rape kit he sent to the lab for tests.

"We'll let you know the results in a day or so."

"Okay. Do you do a pregnancy test as well?" I asked, obviously concerned.

"Not as routinely as ideal. Pregnancy is rare in rape cases, over 98 percent of the time it does not occur. Only 0.3 percent of all abortions are due to rape. If a positive test comes back, we find the child is usually the girl's father's or her boyfriend's child. Most rapists aren't exactly fully normal, sexually. The main worry, by far, is venereal disease, which we always test for first. It's too early for a pregnancy test anyway so you'll need that done in a few weeks or so."

"Yes, you're right. I'm not feeling well now, and am sorry if I don't make much sense."

"Okay. Just relax. You will be fine."

Dr. Beltz then stood up, saying, "I'm going to call Dr. Rivera. Do you know him? He's a psychiatrist here at the hospital."

"Yes, I know him—I know him very well. He works on the floor above me, and we often eat lunch together. His wife was my roommate in college. I have known him since I was hired at the hospital over two years ago."

"Good. I usually do the forensics evaluations, but he is much better at helping persons get through this kind of traumatic experience. It's what he does best." He then phoned Dr. Rivera, and, as soon as someone answered, Dr. Beltz asked, "Dr. Rivera? This is Dennis in the Forensics Department. I have Ms. Rebekah Martin here who just completed an evaluation." Dr. Rivera, obviously concerned, asked, "Why, what happened?"

"She was raped and is very shaken. I have her medicated, and she should not drive. The Fort Worth Police Department has also impounded her car, which is now the crime scene. They didn't want her to contaminate the forensic evidence, you know fingerprints, hair fibers, and such."

Dr. Rivera then answered, "Be over shortly. Things are slow here and most all of the patients are asleep, so I can stop by now to see what I can do to help."

In less than ten minutes, he arrived. As soon as Dr. Rivera got here, he said to me, "You don't look good. You are going home with me. I will call my wife and she will get the spare bedroom ready."

"No, I'm fine. I can just rent a car and drive back to my apartment."

"Oh, no you don't. You don't need an accident on top of the rape!"

"You can drive me home, then, and I will be fine."

"Look. I do not want you to go back to your apartment, not right now. We're friends, as well as colleagues. You and my wife were roommates in college and she would be insulted if I drove you home instead of having you come over to our place to stay."

"You're right, she would be hurt. I would also be hurt, I'm sure. I find her company very comforting, at this time especially. She was like a mother to me in college, even though she was a few months younger than me!"

"I know. She is like a mother to a lot of people, even me!" Dr. Rivera added with a warm smile on his face.

"And I'll call the hospital and get a few days off for you. You need rest and a diversion. Doctor's orders!"

"Thank you, doctor. I really appreciate your help."

"It would be wrong for me to do any less," Dr. Rivera answered confidently.

"Thank you! You know full-well I would do the same to help you," I answered.

"Yes, I do, and you may have to someday. Count on it!"

With that, Dr. Rivera and I were soon at his home in an affluent part of town in contrast to where my apartment was. I felt better being around his wife. She also made me feel good, and, as I look back, I really needed her support at this time. Dr. Rivera was right. This was the best plan for me now. I wonder if I would ever be able to go back to my apartment. I was close to a nervous breakdown and, thanks to his help, I was able to deal with the worst experience in my twenty-three years of life. At the time, I thought this would be the worst event of my life, ever, but more trauma would soon come later.

CHAPTER 2
The Day After

After I was finally exhausted enough to fall asleep, I slept fairly well considering the events of the day. I did wake up several times with panic attacks, and Dr. Rivera said I was screaming in my sleep, "Help! Get off me. You are hurting me! Please help me!" Dr. Rivera then gave me something stronger to help me sleep. It knocked me out cold and I then slept for several hours. The next morning, after I came to, I was able to visit with my college friend, Dr. Rivera's wife, Mindy. We were roommates in nursing school and I felt close to her almost from day one when I first met her in college. I was concerned about what kind of person my roommate would be, a concern due to the horror stories I heard from friends, but it turned out I was worried for no reason. I was blessed with a good friend I still value. Whenever I think of nursing school I also have fond memories of the man, a relative, who paid my way through, David Kline, another good memory. Without his help I would have never been able to afford a top tier college. My father had been ill for years before he passed, my mother died several years ago, and I was struggling financially.

"Did you sleep well?" Mindy asked. "You always did in college, so I hope the medicine my husband gave you helped," showing her usual concern.

"I slept as well as could be expected, given the circumstances," I answered, still somewhat groggy from the medicine, and I, fortunately, could not remember my nightmares. Mindy had to relate them to me.

"If you want to talk about your traumatic ordeal, I'm here for you. And I will not send you a bill, but remember you get what you pay for!" Mindy said, attempting some humor. I didn't appreciate her humor very much, but I greatly appreciated her spirit.

"Actually, I would rather talk to you than anyone in the world, even my pastor." I responded sincerely. But first I need to call my boyfriend again."

"Good idea. Here's the phone," she said, as she handed me the pink princess phone on her desk. I called him and, again, no answer. I thought this was odd, to say the least. So I spent the next hour filling Mindy in about what happened, adding, "Dr. Beltz didn't show much sympathy, and acted like it was just his job. Since he has seen many cases like mine, it was no big deal for him."

"What you needed was to talk to a woman who can relate to what you went through, not a man who can't," Mindy said in her usual kind, supportive voice.

"I agree, although my father was always very emotionally supportive."

"Of course. He was really more our father!" Mindy always liked my father. Both she and I took losing him very hard and felt alone after he died of pancreatic cancer at the young age of forty-seven.

We had a good day talking about our college days, which helped me to take my mind off of the previous day. Dr. Rivera came home for lunch. He lived only a few miles away from the hospital and wanted to spend as much time with his family as possible. When he got home, he gave me some advice.

"We have to find a car for you and, as I thought about it,

you will need to find another place to live. Your apartment is in the worst part of the city of Fort Worth," he stated in his very authoritative Cuban voice.

"Oh. You're right. And thank you for your help," I acknowledged with a smile of appreciation.

"And the memories of that location and your apartment will remind you of that traumatic event. Generally, in dealing with transient stress disorders, you need to be removed from the place and things that remind you of the traumatic event. That means another car and a new apartment."

Mindy then added, "I will take Rebekah around town to look for a good, used, late-model car, and we can continue our girl talk!"

"Good. A friend and I are building some new one-bedroom cottage houses nearby we can look at," Dr. Rivera added as an afterthought.

I also tried to call Robert several times during the day, and again got no answer.

I had no idea when the police department investigation was going to return my car. So, we spent almost two weeks finding a good low-mileage, used car and a new place to live. I decided to rent one of the cottages Dr. Rivera and his co-investors were building. One was close to being ready to move into, so I signed the lease. Dr. Rivera and his brother, who was a lawyer, rented a truck and moved all of my things from the old apartment into my new home. After my two-week medical leave, I returned to work. I was very fortunate to have good friends help me get through this very difficult time of my life. Mindy was especially helpful. She always was!

I finally got ahold of Robert. He said he had been very busy lately. When I told him what had happened, he feigned support, but it was clear at that point that I was a handy girlfriend for a year or so, and he decided to move on to someone else.

"Robert, I called you about eight or ten times, yet you never answered the phone. When I needed you more than any time in my life, you were not there. I was raped and ended up in the hospital."

"I'm sorry. I was very busy."

"Too busy for your girlfriend?"

"I told you, I'm sorry, I really am. I had a lot of things come up." "You could have at least answered the phone!"

"I told you, I was very busy, and I'm very sorry. I really am."

"Well, I will let you go since you are so busy. I can see you are far too busy for me. 'Sorry' does not explain what you did." And then I hung up, furious at his callousness and apathy. Of all the time to lose a boyfriend, just when I really needed him to be supportive! We had some friction about several things before this, so it didn't completely surprise me. I was a perfectionist and he was, at times, messy with household tasks and was a slob as a dresser. When I visited his apartment, it always looked like a pigsty. I thought when I was there that I could not live like that. I'm a neat person, always very fussy about my appearance and my living space. My anger could also be partly because I was mad at a man who I thought was my best friend, my boyfriend; at least I thought he was my boyfriend. I was angry that he was not supportive during this difficult time for me.

After I hung up the phone, I thought to myself, "This was another big disappointment. I liked him a lot in spite of our many differences, but I guess the feeling was not mutual."

Mindy then perceptively noted, at least I hoped she was correct when she told me, "You are a very attractive girl and always had more than your fair share of dates, so now is a good time to move on. You are still young and, in my opinion, he is just not worth it." I later found out later that my boyfriend went back to his old girlfriend several weeks ago and that is why he did not answer the phone when I called him. He was with her and could not answer his phone!

A few days later I got some very good news about the tests done at the forensics lab. No evidence of sexually transmitted disease! I was relieved, very relieved! I was moving forward and looking forward to putting my life back together again . . . without Robert.

CHAPTER 3
Another Trauma Enters

After a few weeks, I don't remember how many, I missed my next period and had some spotting. Since I began menstruating, I occasionally missed a period, mostly when training for track in college. But I was not in training now, so I talked to my doctor about my concerns. I knew a pregnancy test is usually ordered ten days after a woman missed her period. He knew all about my recent rape experience, and said it was likely due to the trauma I had experienced. "Some women occasionally miss their period for no obvious reason," he added. "Don't worry," he reassured me. "You have been through a lot and need to give it a few more weeks to level out."

Soon I noticed my breasts were swollen and tender. Then I noted I was unusually fatigued, and experienced nausea and what I thought was morning sickness. Oh no, I thought. I could be pregnant, a fear my doctor soon confirmed. I'm a trained nurse, so knew I was probably pregnant. Now what do I do?!!

I talked to some friends and colleagues, and they strongly recommended I get an abortion as soon as possible. "Don't wait. The sooner the better," they authoritatively opined.

A colleague firmly told me, "Rape by a man of a different race is more than enough reason to get an abortion. It is allowed even in states that have done everything they can to stop abortions!

Or at least, these states make it as difficult as possible to get an abortion. Rape is one reason for an abortion which, even staunch anti-abortion supporters agree, is a valid reason."

I was told the same thing by several other hospital workers.

Even Dr. Rivera recommended an abortion. "You have gone through enough. If you deliver that child, it will be hard to take care of it as a single working woman. Every time you see it, it will bring back those terrifying memories. No woman should be forced to go through this, ever! You could put it up for adoption, but as an interracial child, good luck!" he said, speaking more sternly than I have ever heard him talk before.

"Not many respectable families will want to adopt that biracial child," he added, clearly stressing the problem. It was the late 1970s and that was still a big issue. I grew up in Detroit and many of my friends were Black, so I frankly did not understand the problem. My best girlfriend was a biracial child. We are still friends, although separated by distance, and she is married to a great man with a young child, so is very busy.

"But I am carrying an innocent child." I protested.

"No, you aren't. At this stage of your pregnancy evolutionists have proven the early embryo passes through the stages in the evolutionary history of our species. At about 30 to 50 days after conception, the developing embryo has the gill slits and gill arches of fish. It even has a caudal appendage labeled a tail in human embryology textbooks. It is not a human," said Dr. Neel, a witness in abortion cases and a visiting professor, who happened to overhear me.

I thought, "Now I need to talk with my pastor." If he agreed, I would take care of this problem with what my friends called a routine medical procedure.

I went in to see Pastor Anderson the next day. He greeted me with his usual hug and invited me into his office.

"What brings you here?" he asked with a warm contagious smile that showed concern, as he usually did when I went in to see him.

"As you know, I was raped and have recently found out that I'm pregnant!"

"I thought it was very unusual to get pregnant from a rape." he stated, sincerely bewildered.

"That's what I was told by my doctor and that's what I learned in nursing school. My doctor said I was one of the lucky ones! I did not appreciate his humor."

"That was uncalled for," Pastor Anderson added.

"Yes, it was, but my doctor later apologized and added, 'The common problem I see is women who are unable to get pregnant, which is a far more common concern.'" In response to this comment, I thought, "What was his point?"

I then added, "My doctor next told me, 'I know this because I have to refer many of my patients to the local fertility clinic.'"

"I can see your doctor's point. What do you want to do?" Pastor Anderson asked.

"I don't know what to do. I'm torn because so many friends are pressuring me to get an abortion, so I thought I would ask you for your advice."

"You know we believe the Scriptures are the foundation of our morality. You are carrying an innocent child of God that has done nothing wrong. But I think that this has to be your decision. I will support you, though, no matter what you decide to do."

"I guess I want you to tell me what to do."

"I believe you already know what to do. Otherwise you wouldn't be asking me. You have a good head on your shoulders and I have confidence that you will make the right decision, the best decision for you and the child."

"And, you need to forgive the rapist, more for your own good than for his. The Scriptures note, reading from his Berean Study Bible, Isaiah 1:18 says, 'Come now, let us reason together," says the LORD: "though your sins are like scarlet, they will be as white as snow; though they are red as crimson, they will become like wool.'"

"Let me give you some background on this scripture." At this point, I knew I was in for a sermon.

"The Hebrew for scarlet refers to an insect, specifically the Coccus ilicis worm, that lodges itself in oak trees. From them comes an ancient red dye. This red color has two meanings, physical and spiritual: Red dye is difficult to remove, as anyone who has tried to do so well knows. Spiritually, such is our sin. We cannot remove it ourselves. So, our sins are nailed to the Cross and, without Jesus, we cannot be made white as wool cloth, meaning our sins forgiven."

In his previous vocation, Pastor Anderson was a biologist, an entomologist actually, so this exposition was not unexpected. I enjoyed his elaborations on the Scriptures. It helped them come alive.

"And remember the two thieves on the Cross? At the time of Jesus' crucifixion two thieves were crucified beside Him. Both at first mocked and blasphemed Him, as did many of the spectators. One of the thieves, however, responded to the salvation message, and Jesus told him, quoting from Luke 23:43, in his favorite translation The Berean Study Bible, 'Truly, I tell you, today you will be with me in paradise.' The second man, guilty and unrepentant, did not respond, and we suspect that he is now suffering from his mistake."

I listened as Pastor Anderson continued, "Remarkably, while in the excruciating torment of the Cross, Jesus had the heart, mind, and will to pray for others. While the disciples were abandoning the Lord, this first man answered the call, and his sins were forgiven, including his blasphemy against the Son of God."

"But a professor at the medical school said the human embryo at the early stage is just a fish, and not a human," I protested. "So it is not really human.

"I taught embryology at the medical school, and I can tell you this once commonly held belief is wrong. The eminent German professor Ernst Haeckel started this idea in the 1800s. Now the

Biogenetic Law, the so-called Recapitulation Theory, has been proven to be fraudulent."

"Fraudulent? How do you know?" I asked, shocked and surprised.

He then pulled out a book titled *Haeckel's Embryos: Images, Evolution, and Fraud*, from his large bookcase and opened it up to a page marked by a large red bookmark. I read the page he marked and was mad. The Biogenetic Law was a fraud, pure and simple.

"I don't blame you for being mad at the myths spread today." He responded, "but they are misleading, no deceiving, us! Falsely misleading us to accept abortion not for what it is, a human." Pastor Anderson added, emphasizing the word 'deceiving'.

"That seems to be true," I added, agreeing.

"But now you will need to forgive the rapist. That is the real challenge." Pastor Anderson added.

"Yes, I know. But that is very difficult. That man ruined my life!"

"Often, in the end, resentment and anger can eat at you and, in the long run, cause more harm than the original offense," he added.

I just sat there wondering how I could forgive this monster as I waited for Pastor Anderson to say something else. After a few minutes, I said I would think more about what he said and, after thanking him, I left. This was the hardest decision I have made in my life. As I thought about it, I realized he was right about one thing. The child was innocent. He or she had done nothing wrong. I felt in my heart that I had to give this child life. But this child was too much wrong--wrong race, wrong color, wrong time. No father, a career mother with no time to give it the love it needed. Every time I would look at it, I felt it would remind me of the worst day in my life.

About this time I received a call from my distant relative, David Kline, who helped me get through nursing school. We had corresponded a lot and he had come to my graduation from nursing school that he paid for, so the phone call didn't surprise me. He told me he had been doing more genealogy research and had more details.

"Really? What did you find?" I inquired, now very curious.

"Lots. I know our exact relationship. My great-grandmother Sara Kline married your great grandfather, Benjamin Aldrich. Guess what, you are ethnically part Jewish!"

"I thought so, given my jet black hair and what you told me in the past."

"The genealogists I hired figured you are about six percent Jewish because your great-grandfather was one-fourth Jewish. I knew you were, but did not know the details."

"That's not all!" David continued.

"And?" I asked, anxious to hear more.

"You are also part African, a very small part but still a part. Your great-great-grandmother was part African. She was a freewoman who lived in England."

"I was what?" I asked, hardly believing what he had just said.

"Not only her, but some of your other relatives were African as well, which is not really all that uncommon for Europeans or Americans."

"Are you sure?"

"Yes, I have a genealogy chart with all of the details and do not want to read it on the phone, so will mail you a copy."

"I had no idea!" I shot back.

"You might wonder why I am calling you out of the blue now."

"Yes, I do."

"I know you are pregnant with a half African American child, and you should know your heritage."

"What?"

"You are pregnant with a half African American child, and you should know your heritage. I know that because you may remember you briefly told me about your situation."

"I heard you. I just have to try to process what you just told me."

"We are all children of Adam and Eve, all related, all brothers and sisters. I am quoting from the Hebrew Scriptures. You just have a little more blood from the other side of the family than most others. Think about this."

"If costs are a concern I would be honored to cover all of the expenses. I want you to have that baby!" David stressed to get his point across.

"No, I have good insurance, but your call has forced me to look at my situation very differently."

"As you know I am raising my son, Billy, as a Christian. I am now convinced that Jesus was the Biblical Messiah."

"Yes, you mentioned that to me before, but religion is not my concern now," I added wondering why he would bring this up.

"I know that, but I can encourage Billy and live by example and I hope I can be an example for you as well."

"I appreciate that, I really do." I answered with a crooked half smile on my face.

David then told me he would mail the genealogy report and we said our goodbyes. I always felt good when I talked to him.

My thought as I hung up was that he was a very good and wonderful man, who by his presence has made the world a much better place.

I would soon hear from his son Billy. It seems I was someone who he could relate to, someone he could trust.

CHAPTER 4
My Problematic Pregnancy

As time went on, it became increasingly obvious that I was pregnant. As I became larger, occasionally comments by others came back to me, like "I guess it's too late now for an abortion but I'm sure you could get two doctors to agree in your case that an abortion is necessary for your mental health. After all, this child is the result of rape and it will remind you of that terrifying event every time you look at it."

Fortunately, such comments were now less common, but nonetheless they hurt when I occasionally heard them. One time a colleague noted, "I have a good friend who runs an adoption agency, and I can make an appointment for you if you like."

"I appreciate the help, but I plan on keeping this child."

"Are you sure?" he asked with a quizzical look on his face.

"Yes, I'm sure. Very sure." Inside I was not so sure. It would be nice to hear some encouragement from others, at least occasionally, but the academic culture I was part of, the hospital I worked at was part of the university, believed I should abort it and get on with my life.

I had also dated Dr. Albert Bass, a professor at the university that my hospital was associated with. After he put pressure on me to abort, I realized things were not going to work out between us, although I really liked him. We had some great times together.

"As a single, very attractive educated woman, you are in a good position to marry well," he opined in a way that reminded me of academics who analyzed everything.

"That all may be true, but if a man will not respect me in this decision, the most important decision I have made in my life, I don't think it will work out," I told him, which made him angry.

"What about my belief?" he added.

"I respect your thoughts," I told Dr. Bass, "but what about my thoughts? I'm the one carrying this child," I added, disappointed in Albert.

These comments, and rejections, as rare as they were, led me to pray often, asking God to be with me and the child, and to affirm that I had made the right decision. I sure wondered if I did, but knew regardless that having this baby was not going to be easy. Pastor Anderson at church last week assured me I was making the correct decision, even though I was bucking what seemed to be the academic consensus.

After being ignored by some of my coworkers whose actions showed me, by what I interpreted as shunning, that they did not agree with my decision, a staff doctor, Dr. Mwangi, took me aside one day and said, "I'm proud of your decision to carry your child to term. You are doing the right thing. In my country, we believe a child is the most precious gift on Earth, and we would never abort a child, even one conceived by rape. This is our culture. In addition, we are Christians. Our religion in this case strongly supports my African culture," he explained as he put his hand on my arm as a sign of reassurance. He was from Nairobi, Kenya.

"Oh, I could add in all 300 major dialects in Africa there is no word for killing an unborn child. I learned the word abortion in America, and had to ask what it meant," he noted.

I felt good about his support, very good, and told him so. "Thank you! You don't know how important your kind words are to me," I responded, genuinely appreciating his support. Those few kind words made a great difference that day, and in the days afterward as well.

"Dr. Mwangi. A few thoughtful supportive words mean so much to me at this time." I added.

After about eight months since I found out I was pregnant, I found myself in the delivery room alone, since Robert, and it seemed almost everyone else, had abandoned me. I knew Professor Albert Bass would not be there, which reinforced my opinion about him. I told him just a few days prior when I was due that it would be nice if he came to support me. He said he would try. "Sure!" I thought to myself.

After a few hours, I heard the nurse say in a loud voice, "She has dilated to ten centimeters. Ask the doctor to come in now."

"I will be there very shortly," the doctor responded in his deep radio announcer voice.

CHAPTER 5

A Child Is Born

I then saw Dr. Mwangi walk into the delivery room. I felt very supported! After he said hi, he added, "I wanted you to have the best care possible. I'm proud to be part of this delivery to see this beautiful baby come into the world." I found out later that Dr. Mwangi had arranged several specialists to be on call if problems developed. None did but, he said, "Just in case."

I felt good that he was there. Neither my old boyfriend, nor my most recent guy friend, were, but one of the best doctors in the hospital was here with me! I felt enormously blessed.

After a fairly easy delivery, Dr. Mwangi announced, "It's a girl! A beautiful, brown-skinned girl with a head of Shirley Temple curly hair, only jet black!"

After the umbilical cord was cut, she was cleaned and prepped. I then held her and felt wonderful. She was absolutely gorgeous! I knew then that I made the right decision. And I was never to regret it. Never. She would eventually change my life in ways I could never imagine.

After several weeks at home to recuperate, with Mindy by my side much of the time mothering me and my baby, I visited the hospital where I worked to show off my joy. I expected the worst but was very pleasantly surprised!

"What a beautiful child! Let me hold her! Isn't she precious!" Marie, my supervisor, gushed.

"Oh, let me hold her," the charge nurse voiced with excitement, as she put her arms out to hold what she called my "bundle of joy."

They repeatedly complimented her about her beautiful brown skin, brown eyes, and her jet-black head of Shirley Temple hair.

"You know," Marie added, "that brown skin will reduce the likelihood of skin cancer, not just basal cell carcinoma but also especially the dangerous kind, melanoma."

"I'm very aware of this because I had a cousin that died of melanoma. It was not on her back, as is common, but the back of her leg, so she never noticed it until it had metastasized and it was then too late," I added, agreeing with Marie.

Although I did not carry the baby to full term for the benefit of my coworkers, it felt good, no, actually wonderful, to get their approval. And it turned out she was a good baby, not average, nor difficult as I had expected. Even Robert came by later to see her, but he was as ice-cold as could be. I heard he was not getting along with his old, . . . sorry, . . . his new girlfriend. Too bad! I am moving on.

I had made the right decision and now thoroughly enjoyed being a mother. In fact, I was in heaven in my role as a mother. I was able to go back to work after three weeks and two days. Mindy helped me watch my baby, which I then named Zawadi, a Swahili word which means gift. Dr. Mwangi suggested the name. He told me it was pronounced Zaa-WAA- Diy! in answer to she turned out to be a pure joy. And she was a pure joy. Her middle name was Marie, the same as mine, named after my grandmother.

In the end, after most people could not pronounce her suggested moniker, but also because she was an angel, I named her Angela Marie Martin. Her first name was now Angela and when we found out her father's surname much later, we had her last name changed on the birth certificate. I don't know why I did that. I guess my Christian faith said she needed a father, if only on paper. But that is another story.

This little girl changed my life for the better. The day she was born turned out to be the best day of my life, no question! I was never to reject my decision not to abort her, ever.

Later, Dr. Mwangi stopped by to see how we were doing. He was very fatherly, and still very protective of me and my child. He mentioned one of his concerns was abortion, noting that "abortion is a greater cause of death for Blacks than heart disease, cancer, diabetes, AIDS, and violence combined. About 40 to 50 percent of all Black babies are aborted each year."

I was stunned by these statistics and told him so.

"Allow me to add that Margaret Sanger, who led the revolution that resulted in the Planned Parenthood empire, was specifically concerned about reducing the population of "less fit" humans, including, especially African Americans. As Sanger stressed, the end goal of her movement was to produce a superior race by eugenics, meaning the use of evolution to make superior humans."

David Kline also called and told me he sent a nice check so I could go out and buy some baby clothes and other things I needed. To save money most of what I needed I bought at the local Goodwill.

Life was very ordinary for a couple of years. I took care of my Angela, went to church, dated a few guys whom, it seems, did not really want to marry a ready-made family, especially with a Black child. None of my suitors told me this, I just suspected it. I also just never met the guy of my dreams. I did a few things with Dr. Rivera and Mindy, but my focus was on my daughter and her life, and also my career.

In the meantime, after Angela was three, the headlines of the local paper announced that a rapist who had murdered his last victim, Susie Tompkins, was to go to trial soon. Shortly after the paper's announcement I received a call from the Fort Worth prosecutor's office.

"We are trying to clear a backlog of rape and murder cases, and so checked your rape kit. We found a perfect match! Yours and several others.

"We may want you to testify in court. We probably will not need you to testify, but, just in case, please keep us informed of your whereabouts."

The prosecutor then added "Oh. Let me add, we have indisputable DNA evidence of the murdered woman, so may not need you to testify. Testifying in these cases is most always traumatic for the women, so we do not want to put you through it if we do not have to."

"I appreciate that. I really do. I expect it would be very traumatic for me, but I will testify if I need to."

"Thank you for your willing cooperation! We really appreciate all the support we can get."

I then added, "If the court needs my help, I will be honored to do what I can to convict this danger to society and get him off the streets for good. Just ask."

I did not think much about it then, but later I remembered the call. It would change my life again in ways I never expected. Never.

CHAPTER 6

Convicted of Rape and Murder

I t turned out, as we expected, the jailed suspect was convicted by DNA evidence of both rape and murder. In Texas, the hanging state, he was given the death penalty. One woman who was part of the local NOW (National Organization for Women) organization testified for the prosecutor. We saw parts of the sentencing phase on television. "So, what is your opinion?" the prosecutor asked her.

"There's no question that this violence is against all women, and this convicted murderer must pay, and pay severely for his crime as an example to others. Every man's wife, daughter, sister and mother demands it. There is no worse possible offense. None. The death penalty must be instituted to send a message to all men who even think about committing this crime."

After several more testimonies along this line, Susie Tompkins's family testified. Her husband was especially dramatic, showing a great deal of emotion over the loss of his wife and his children's mother.

"I lost my love, my best friend, my wife, my two children's mother. Her parents, her brother, her uncles and aunts all lost her. She was the joy of our life. We are devastated. We lost Susie Tompkins for no good reason, only because of this perverted man. This sick man who should never ever be able to walk the streets as a free man again."

After pausing to let what he just said sink in, her widower then added, "Susie Tompkins was a good mother, deeply loved her children. She was a school teacher, fully dedicated to her chosen profession. That rapist Turner has ruined the lives of so many people. I demand the death penalty! Nothing less will do. The Bible says 'an eye for an eye and a tooth for a tooth' and I believe that is the moral, as well as the right, thing to do."

I didn't know all of the details of this murder but in some ways, I got off easy. In my case no one lost their wife, their mother, their daughter or their best friend . . . although I did lose Robert. I found out later he heard about the rape from his police scanner that he regularly listened to, I guess for excitement. Needless to say, after watching this news clip, I had several sleepless nights. I did not want to be reminded of the worst day in my life.

CHAPTER 7
Preschool

Always a vivacious little girl, and because Mindy started working part-time, I enrolled my daughter in a preschool. Angela was very shy, but soon fit in perfectly. For the past three years Angela accumulated accolades from almost everyone. Sorry, *definitely* from everyone! She was clearly a very bright girl, very articulate and outgoing, now that she finally adjusted to daycare.

I remember a girl her age asked my daughter what happened to her skin because it was so dark. Angela shot back with, "Well, what happened to your skin that made it so light?"

Later, one of the mothers told me that Angela said I, her mother, became so light-skinned because I used too much bleach to bleach the clothes I washed and, as a result, my skin got lighter and lighter as time went on!

Then a topic less humorous came up. One day she came home from preschool and, again, asked about her father. I found out that the children had brought in their fathers to meet the class on Father's Day. Most all of the children had fathers they could bring in to show off with pride to the class. For this reason, Angela became even more aware of a father's role in a little girl's life. When she asked about her father, I was again very evasive. "I told you that your father lived very far away." What else could I say?

"How far away?" Angela asked.

"Many miles away."

"How many miles?"

"How many miles?" Angela had asked again. I now felt I had to tell her something and I was not going to lie about her father. What exactly to tell her was the main question.

As her asking about her father became more frequent, I realized my evasiveness was only causing more problems.

After she said to me, "When can I see my father! You said I could, and you lied to me!" The tears now f lowed as she kicked me in the shins. She had never done that before, so it was clear that I had to do something, but what could I do?

"Is my Dad dead?"

"No, he is not dead."

"Then why can't I see him?" Angela asked, still crying.

"I will see if I can arrange a visit with him," I told her to stall her yet again about this question. I knew I could not put it off forever. I had to tell her the truth someday, but not just yet.

She was really taking this hard so I decided to talk to Pastor Anderson.

"Well, how are you doing?" he asked.

"Not so good," I answered. I then added some details to what had happened.

"I suggest that you try to visit her father in prison. I know that will be difficult, but my thought is, in this case you need to put your daughter first."

"If I do, I will bring a gun with me!"

"If you do, you couldn't get into the prison!"

"I know, but that's what I feel like doing."

"I suggest you take the high road. He is on death row, he may well die for what he did. Isn't that enough punishment?"

"Frankly, no."

"Well, as the scriptures say, 'Vengeance is mine, says the Lord.'"

"You always have a scripture for everything."

"Not everything, but I have learned the hard way that scripture admonition usually turns out to be excellent advice. You do need to get over your anger. It's hurting you and not him."

"I guess you are right." I acknowledged to him. My feeling was that Pastor Anderson is a man, and so does not know what it's like to be sexually assaulted.

"At least talk to the warden. You know, he is a member of our congregation."

"Yes, I know."

As the prison warden, Ronald Arber, attended our church, I agreed I should visit him. So to keep my promise to Angela I did the very next week.

Later at church I walked up to him and said, "Warden Arber, I need to talk to you about my daughter. I learned the DNA test I gave as part of the rape investigation proved my child was fathered by Trevon Turner, the convicted rapist."

"Please, Rebekah, call me Ron."

"Thank you, Ron. As you know, I was raped over four years ago by Turner."

"Yes, and, as you must know, I am very aware of this case. It's my job to be aware of a lot of events that deal with the prison and the prisoners!"

"My daughter, Angela, wants to meet her dad. Is this possible? Advisable? What are your thoughts?"

I then added, "Please be honest with me. I need to know the best approach."

"I will be honest. I have always strongly recommended that children get to know their fathers, even those fathers in here who are serving life sentences, and, yes, even those on death row, as Trevon Turner is now. Often their sentences get commuted, and those on death row end up serving life in prison."

"What about Trevon Turner?"

"He has a very good record and it would not surprise me if

his sentence was commuted. I thought he had a good reason that explained why Susie Tompkins died. The fact is, this does not excuse his behavior in the least, as you know, but it helps me to understand the mind of this rapist."

"I don't really care to understand them." I responded. "I want to forget him, but have to put my daughter first, above everything."

"It helps you to deal with what happened if you understand why they rape. Anger towards his mother, or some woman in his life, some believe, partly explains it. Or the loss of their father when young."

"All this was interesting, but only part of what I wanted to know" I explained, interrupting him.

"I want to add that Black males between 12 and 45 are only four percent of the population in America and, in most prisons, including ours, they are close to seventy percent of the prison population. In our prison, the majority of the African-American inmates come from homes lacking a father or appropriate male model. In the U.S., about seventy percent of African American males are reared by their mothers or grandmothers. The fathers are too often not part of the picture. This is a major problem, and we see the results in our prisons. And this is why I'm very supportive of doing what I can to make sure fathers in here can still be a male role model, even those who have done very evil crimes like Trevon."

"What I want to know now is, why did he kill her? That seems unspeakably cruel to me," I pressed.

"The story we got was he had the gun and she struggled, and tried to grab the gun away from him. It went off and shot her in the head. The next day she was found dead in her car in the parking lot near where she lived."

He then added, "Trevon was seen throwing the gun in a nearby river by a man in a five-story building nearby, and that man called the police. He also got the license number of the car, and, as a result Trevon was caught. The gun was registered to him and ballistics tests matched the gun to him. He confessed, and actually told the police he was glad he was caught since he had a compulsion to rape. Only prison would stop his raping, Trevon added. As a matter of fact, this response is not all that rare. He was convicted on the forensics evidence alone. The ballistic and DNA evidence was conclusive. This is why you did not need to testify."

Then Ron thought for a few seconds, lifted his head up, and began speaking again.

"I should add, he voluntarily gave saliva for the DNA test without a second thought. He seemed to want to get convicted without a long trial involving the victims. We did not need any more evidence."

"Then it was an accident?"

"Legally, in this state it doesn't matter if it was an accident. If someone dies, even accidently, when committing a felony, you are guilty of capital murder. Period. Another side is he could have shot her in the head so she could not testify against him in court, and just claimed it was an accident, but I believe his story, which is just my judgment, and could be wrong."

I added, "Thank you for your thoughts. I have tried to read about this topic to understand why rapists do what they do. It is baffling to me, to say the least. I have even read about rapists that apologize to the victim for their crime before they leave. Others are sadistic and seem determined that the victim suffers as much as possible for no reason except cruel sadism."

"I appreciate your understanding, Ms. Martin. I have learned that rape victims meeting with the rapist can be very traumatic and adversely affect their mental health. Or, on the other hand, it can help the victim overcome the common, but unhealthy, self-defeating hate against the offender. As you know, the anger against the offender, and demanding revenge, can hurt the victim, yes victim, greatly and has little effect on the offender. The Christian response is to forgive, not seven times, but up to seventy-times-seven times. The victim's seething hate can, in the long run, do more harm than the offense itself," Ron explained as he raised his hands to emphasize his point.

Then, looking at Warden Arber, I asked, "So, in my case, your recommendation is?"

"Let me do some checking with the psychological staff here, and I will let you know my decision. The therapists here get to know the offenders fairly well. They are fooled at times by so-called 'jail house conversions,' but generally their assessments are accurate."

"I really appreciate your support. I have had to struggle with this ever since Angela was born. I think I will have to come to grips with what that evil man did, but do not know how best to handle my daughter's dilemma. She really wants to see her father and, ideally, to get to know him as a father. You know I have not married since then, and part of the problem is this issue."

"Well, thank you for your visit. I will get to this posthaste and let you know Sunday in church. I'm a very unorthodox warden, but my innovation exploits have allowed me to develop a good reputation, mostly because I have managed to make what turned out to be some very good decisions. I believe rules are guidelines and each individual case has to be considered on its merits."

After our mutual thanks, I left feeling very good. I was still very ambivalent about meeting this man. How would I react? Would it bring back the horrible memories of that terrible, frightening night? But I had to put my daughter first and knew she needed to meet her father. At least we had to try.

In church Sunday, Warden Arber said, "It's a go," then he added, "You need to meet him first and feel out his perceptions and feelings about meeting his daughter."

CHAPTER 8

Meeting the Man Who Caused Me So Much Pain

I t was arranged for me to meet him next Wednesday. I was to meet him in the secure visitor's area. I was a nervous wreck and could not stop shaking, even after swallowing a Xanax. After the guard let me in, he said, "You have fifteen minutes with Trevon and you are not to pass anything across the bars. You will be watched for the entire time on video."

After he was brought into the screened visiting area I did not recognize him, but said hi. He just looked at me. I knew it must have been him. Who else could it be? He also seemed to have no idea who I was. "Are you from the press?" he asked.

"No, I'm not," I answered. I thought I must get to the reason I'm here now. "See this picture?" I was careful not to give it to him. "This little girl is your daughter."

He looked at me like I was out of my mind.

"My daughter? I don't have a daughter." He then looked at the picture closely, obviously intrigued, but said nothing.

"Do you remember the night by the Hillard Apartments on the south side of Fort Worth? I had a red 1974 Chevy. You had a gun. You told me not to scream, so I would not get hurt."

He stared at me intensely, wide-eyed, and said nothing.

Then he said, "What do you want? Money? I don't have any money. I'm in prison, if you haven't noticed."

"I don't want your money. I want you to meet your daughter."

"I told you, I don't have a daughter. Please leave, and leave me alone! I have no idea who you are and what you are talking about."

"I had DNA tests done. Here is the report," which I then showed to him. He just stared at it.

"I also had your last name put on her birth certificate because you are her father." I then showed it to him.

"How do you know this girl is my child?" he asked.

"There's no question that you are the father. I was a virgin and DNA tests proved you are the father. No one else could be. It's impossible." I knew that he was very aware of DNA testing because DNA was critical in convicting him.

"What do you really want?" he asked again.

"I told you, I want you to meet your daughter. That's all."

"What if I don't want to?"

That set me off.

"Look, you had a gun to my head and now things have reversed. I now have a gun to your head. I know the warden and I can get you put in solitary if you refuse to cooperate. You are going to meet your daughter and be nice to her, do you understand?" I was obviously going a little beyond what Warden Arber recommended, but I was angry. I guess I expected this man would welcome seeing his daughter. I was very naïve.

I ended with, screaming in his face, "Think about it. Solitary is not pleasant, but you already know that." Our first meeting was not exactly friendly.

About this time, fortunately, the guard was back. I asked him if I could give the picture of his daughter to him. The guard took it, looked at it, felt the thickness of the picture, and said with a smile on his face, "Sure, pictures of kids are okay."

So, I gave it to him and told him I would be back a week

from that today during visiting hours. I then left. I had tried to get him to take some responsibility for his daughter, and had no idea how this would turn out. If it didn't turn out well, I thought I would tell Angela the whole horrible story and let the chips fall where they may.

CHAPTER 9

Back to the Prison

I was back on time and Trevon was waiting for me. That was a good sign. I said hi, and he said hi to me. I got a good report from the warden who talked to him about his responsibilities. This time I had Angela with me. She stared at him for what seemed like a minute or two. He stared back. Angela smiled and asked, "Are you my father?" He said, "Yes, I am." I then breathed a huge sigh of relief! We made it this far!! I also said another silent prayer or two.

I later learned that the warden had a long talk with him, explaining that things would go a lot better for him if he accepted the fact that Angela was his daughter. If he didn't, things would not go nearly as well. He understood very well what he should do. He was not ignorant and had learned how to survive in prison thus far. The warden had a lot of experience with inmates and their children. And I mean a lot!"

Angela then said out of the blue in her sweet, childish voice, "I love you." Trevon just smiled.

Angela then asked him, "What do you do all day here?"

"I used to spend a lot of time in my room, but now I have been able to work in the wood shop with some very talented wood workers. I have always liked to work with wood. I find it is really enjoyable and very relaxing. I make things for the people here and for my friends, the ones I have left."

"I will be your friend," Angela offered.

"I really appreciate that. Friends are the most important thing in the world." Trevon added.

I was thrilled with how things were going so far. I then said another silent prayer, this time of thanks.

"Can you go home soon?" Angela then asked. "Maybe, if I behave," Trevon answered.

Angela just sat there waiting for Trevon to say something.

"I miss home and my brother and mother. They are very good people. I can see that now," Trevon added.

"My mom told me she gave you a picture of me. Do you still have it?" Angela asked.

"Of course I do! I treasure it. It is on the wall of my room and I have shown it to my friends in the prison, and they said, 'You must be very proud of your daughter.' I said to them, 'most certainly I am. Wouldn't any father be proud of her?'"

I thought he may be trying to get off of death row and earning some brownie points by his behavior, or maybe he just didn't want to spend time in solitary confinement. I even thought, hoped actually, that he was telling the truth. I really wanted him to be honest. Prisoners are very good at lying. After more small talk the guard told us our fifteen minutes were up and Angela told her dad she loved him.

We said our goodbyes and I told him, "We will see you next Wednesday." I think he was genuinely touched by her. Who wouldn't be? She was a beautiful, charming little girl. Everyone was charmed by her! I was, of course, very biased about my daughter.

I then told Angela, "We had a good meeting with your father, didn't we?"

"Yes, we did! I love my Daddy!" she added.

He sure wasn't the kind of person I expected a convicted rapist and murderer to be like, but I was sure he was playing the game just to get off of death row. At least that's what I thought. Before we left, he asked for a full-sized picture of Angela. I said I had several and would bring him one. He seemed sincere, but I felt if Angela could develop a good relationship with her father, I was happy. My concern was for her, not for him or me. I had power over him and he knew it. This was a very good feeling for me. Finally, revenge! After I thought this, it hit me that my pastor encouraged forgiveness. I still couldn't see how I could forgive him for what he did to me and many other women. How could any woman?

Angela then added, "My father is a nice man! He has dark skin like me, even much darker than me!"

As I drove home, I thought, "So far, I am very happy with how things are going!" Actually, I was ecstatic!

CHAPTER 10

The Visits Continue Making Progress

The next week, Angela brought some of her schoolwork drawings to show to her father. I had to admit she had some artistic talent for a four-year-old. Her teachers even noted to me that she had a real talent and recommended I encourage her to develop her exceptional skills in this area. They looked more like drawings by a much older girl. We got permission to give her drawings to her father. It also seemed to me that in each visit we had more and more privileges, such as our fourth visit was twenty minutes long, not just fifteen as before. I assumed this was because the trust factor had increased. Trevon also found some jokes to help pass the time.

"Where do you find a dog with no legs?"

Angela just looked at her father and had no idea, but said, "In his doggy bed?"

"No. Right where you left him! Remember he has no legs!"

She thought that one was tricky, but when the answer sunk in she giggled in her sweet voice.

"Why did the picture go to jail?"

"Because he did something wrong?" Angela answered.

"No. It was framed! Remember a picture frame?" She got that one right away.

"Why did the chicken cross the playground?"

"To get to the other slide!" Angela answered. She had heard that joke before and smiled when she answered.

"What can you catch but not throw?"

That really stumped her. After a few minutes Angela answered correctly, "A cold!"

I had to wonder if she actually figured that one out on her own. Even I didn't know the answer!

"What has hands but can't clap?" Angela was lost. So her dad said, "A clock!"

"What falls in winter but never gets hurt?"

Angela got that one after thinking about it, answering confidently, "The snow." I couldn't figure that one out either! This exchange helped me to realize how perceptive she was. After another good visit we left looking forward to the next visit.

In church on Sunday, Warden Arber mentioned, "Trevon is sure enamored with Angela. Her picture is prominently displayed in his cell and he brags about her a lot. He also makes the other inmates a little jealous, but who cares! It surprises many outsiders, but the fact is, a lot of the inmates sincerely love their family like any other father."

"That's good to hear!" I added, as I asked him if we could meet in the open meeting room. A guard would be there, so we would be protected. The room we were meeting in was separated by a glass partition with a slot to pass pictures and notes to each other. In this room my daughter couldn't even touch her father. Warden Arber said that it could be arranged to meet in the open meeting room. In our next visit, the meeting was in the general visitor meeting room for trusted inmates.

"Hi, Trevon! I see we have permission to meet in here!"

"Yes, we do," Trevon said, as he grabbed his daughter and gave her a big hug. She was delighted. I now saw Trevon's height. He was over six feet tall and had a body-build like a football player. I wondered if he had never got involved in crime if he would have done well in some sport. I also wondered why he raped women. He surely had had a wide choice of female company. He was that good-looking. I know rape is complex, and related more to aggression against women or society than sex, at least that's what I have read, but I still have to wonder. I still seemed to be pre-occupied with his crime, and not him as a person.

While on this visit, both Angela and Trevon seemed to have a great time. He would tickle her, and she screamed with delight. Reminds me of how my father and I used to play. I had a wonderful father, and not a day goes by where I don't think of him—warm thoughts always. That may be why I so much want my daughter to have a good relationship with her father. It appears that she does.

I told Trevon "I finally brought a full-length picture of Angela for you. I couldn't find a good one the last few times we visited, but I have one now."

"Thanks!! That is a great picture. I really appreciate your effort. It will go up in my room right next to the head shot of her."

Trevon brought several children's board games that he and Angela played. One of the other inmates who had children loaned them to Trevon. I could see he genuinely enjoyed playing five-year-old games with her.

On the next visit, Trevon had found more jokes for Angela. Even I enjoyed hearing them.

"Why do firemen wear red suspenders?"

Angela thought and said, "Because fire trucks are red?"

"No. To keep their pants from falling down!"

Angela laughed hysterically at this joke. I saw nothing funny about it, but I'm an adult and remember I loved hearing these jokes when I was a five- or six-years old.

She enjoyed these jokes. I guess we all did at age five. What I loved was watching her have such a wonderful time with her dad. I have never seen her so happy. She clearly bonded with her father, as I did with my father.

On the next visit, Trevon brought some picture-card pairs and the person had to find what was missing on one picture by comparing the two cards, the master and the copy which was missing something.

"So, what is missing?" Trevon asked.

I don't see anything missing."

"Nothing? Are you sure? Look carefully." She just sat there.

"Look at the face in both pictures and tell me what is missing."

All of a sudden, she started to giggle hysterically. "The mouth is missing!"

"Not the mouth, but the lips."

"Yes, I see it now. This is very funny!"

Once she got the hang of it, she loved the game. It helped her to be more observant. The time went by all too fast and soon after Angela and Trevon said their "I love you's and we departed. It was wonderful watching them have such a great time.

Soon we were meeting on all four visitation days, one hour each, and the guards were somewhat lenient. A ritual soon developed. When leaving, Trevon would say, "See you later alligator" and Angela would smile brightly and respond with "After a while crocodile!" Then he later added, "In an hour, sunflower!"

Somehow, she never tired of this salutation and giggled every time it was said like it was the first time she heard it.

One time, Angela asked me, "When can Daddy come home to live with us?"

All I could say was, "We will see. You must be patient."

"But when?" Angela asked with a puzzled look on her face.

"I don't know." I repeated, thinking about Warden Arber's hope that his sentence would be commuted to life in prison, and visits somewhere else could be arranged. I was still very much an optimist in spite of what happened.

CHAPTER 11

A Surprise

The next week Trevon had a wood carving of Angela based on the picture I gave him!

"Here, this is for you!" he said pridefully.

"For me?" Angela said, as Trevon handed the wood carving to her. She looked at it, and said, "Is this me?"

"Yes, it is you! You're very beautiful!"

Angela absolutely beamed at the carving and I don't blame her. I had never seen anything like it in my life.

"Did you make it?"

"Yes," but he humbly added that he had help from a woodcarver who is there in the prison; but it's still amazing. I looked at it in absolute wonderment! A perfect replica of Angela! She was flattered, as was I. It was made out of red oak and stained with a light brown stain that perfectly matched her skin color.

They then talked about their respective days, Angela about her pre-school adventures and Trevon about his woodworking. I was amazed at watching them interact just like my father and I did. Our allotted time was now over an hour, but it went by so fast that I thought of asking for more time.

Trevon always had a few children's jokes which Angela loved. I think he had a book full of them he got from the prison library.

Before we left he asked her "What did one wall say to the other wall?"

Angela just looked at Trevon and said she had no idea.

"I'll meet you at the corner!" Trevon answered.

Angela thought a minute and then said "Oh, I get it," and again laughed hysterically.

"Why do bees have sticky hair?"

"Give up? Because they use honeycombs!" He had to explain that one to her.

"Can a kangaroo jump higher than the Empire State Building?"

"No, they cannot jump that high. I read about the Empire State Building in school and learned it is one of the tallest buildings in America!" Angela answered.

"The answer is, yes because buildings can't jump at all. They have no legs and besides this are way too heavy!"

Angela also thought about it for a minute and said, "Oh, I get it now!"

After Sunday church, we had a brunch and I had a chance to talk to Warden Arber. He explained Trevon was doing great, adding that we could take an hour and a half for the next family visit.

"Sometimes it works out, but sometimes not, and it is hard to say why. Some men are so maladjusted and their families are so angry at them that it never could work out. In your case, the three of you were all effectively working to ensure it worked out. And, in your case, it worked out exceptionally well. I have been observing you so I can judge your progress. I know you had a very bad first experience with Trevon but you seem to have put this behind you, at least partly."

"I had a horrible experience but, look, I have to suppress my emotions for my, sorry, our child. It's like Trevon is a different person. I now see him as a loving father and not as a murderer, which I know legally he is."

After thinking a few seconds, I continued "To be honest, I had a very difficult time at first dealing with him. I was as mad as I have ever been in my life and wanted to shoot him with a gun when I first met him, but I had to keep my anger in."

"This change isn't rare," Warden Arber added. "I have seen some evil men change when their spouse and children are around. I have also seen many evil men remain evil no matter who is around. There are many very good men in here, which surprises most people. I'm always amazed at how some basically good men do evil things in one area. Usually it's when drinking and/or drugs are involved, or were a contributor to the crime. Rape is a mystery to me, a Dr. Jekyll and Mr. Hyde split. I know in a prison environment some of them do very well. Trevon is one of the best inmates we have now."

As usual, the next visit worked out as well. I was even getting more comfortable around Trevon. This experience certainly helped our daughter, but also helped me overcome my anger and bitterness as well which I knew I needed to do for my own health. At our next church brunch, Warden Arber explained to me, "In my long experience, many offenders grow out of their proclivities, such as rape.

After he rubbed his chin, thinking, he added "More accurately, they lose the desire or compulsion. Thus, for most inmates, common ways of ending recidivism are death, as is obvious, but also maturity, marriage, family, and religious conversion are common reasons. Trevon has experienced three of these benchmarks. As he has told his therapist, he simply has lost the desire to rape. He has grown out of it, and now looks back at it as a distant past of what he once was. He now has a new purpose in life, his daughter. He looks forward to seeing her and actually, as you have noted, prepares for her visit by planning fun things to do with her. It is the highlight of his week. Prison is not exactly a fun time for most inmates. This insight is, ironically, especially true of murderers."

"I have certainly seen the fruits of his preparation. He is like a teacher, always plans ahead with something of interest to do. I also have to wonder about the mother-male and father-female bond."

"You are correct," Warden Arber added. "The opposite-sex bonds of parents and children are often very strong. Mothers often spoil their sons, and fathers their daughters. Adult success for daughters is often due to the father and, of sons, due to their mother, so that works in favor for Trevon and Angela."

"You must have been a psychology major in college!" I added.

"How could you tell?" Warden Arber said, beaming with pride at his knowledge.

CHAPTER 12
The Appeals Run Out

I wanted to know more about the crime that got Trevon life and the death penalty. Since another similar convicted rapist I read about only got life in prison, I asked Warden Arber to look up his case. He found the similar case I read about where the accused didn't get the death penalty.

"It is not clear what happened in this case, in contrast to Trevon's case. It was cold when this offense occurred, in her car, in her garage, with the garage door closed and the engine on. The victim was drunk or on drugs. She could have died of carbon monoxide poisoning. Her body wasn't discovered until a month later, so it was hard to tell exactly when and why she died. The prosecutor's office charged the man involved with both rape and murder. They overcharge, then can get the offender to cop a plea to the charge they wanted in the first place. In Trevon's case, the tests showed she was raped and DNA proved who did it. Legally, the details don't matter. He was guilty of murder."

"I don't understand. Maybe she died due to her drug use? How about Trevon's case? It seems it was accidental. He didn't mean to kill the woman, Susie Tompkins. The gun went off accidently."

"Let me explain again. If you drive the getaway car of a bank robber and someone in the bank is shot and dies or the robber killed the clerk, the car driver is legally responsible as well. If he squeals on the bank robber, he may get a lesser punishment, but could still be charged with murder, and probably will be. Trevon was convicted in part for his earlier record which was proven in court. A good attorney may be able to keep his past out of the trial, but Trevon only had a court-appointed attorney, and he was an African American, so his colloquial goose was cooked!"

Now that I knew more about Trevon and his background, I strongly favored life in prison, and not execution. There was no reason to take him away from his daughter. I moved from hating him to feeling sorry for him. He had also adjusted very well in prison, and was doing very well in his prison job, earning his keep, or at least part of it. We had also seen him mature and grow beyond his irresponsible self and he appeared to have lost his compulsion, which the psychologist stated was part of his rape problem. One of the prison therapists speculated that Trevon saw what he interpreted was a very erotic movie about rape which affected him when he was about twelve. Often a certain significant experience like this can have a profound effect on sexual orientation. Early experiences are critical, even rape in the case of men in their twenties, raping teenage-or-younger boys.

I also became acquainted with one of the key witnesses involved in the appeal. He explained his bad experience to me.

After I had prepared extensively to testify in Trevon's re-trial, his court-appointed attorney was appointed to be a judge, and Trevon's case had to begin over again with another attorney. I had to inform his new attorney about the details of the case, which I had to repeat in detail each time a new attorney was appointed for Trevon. Three times in this case! As is his right, he never got his day in court beyond the first sham trial, nor did I have a chance to present my exculpatory findings. The witnesses who were to testify at his re-trial never did.

The next week Warden Arber contacted me with some of the details of the procedure. "After waiting, the court decided to skip the retrial. They concluded there was nothing that would change it even though the key witness possessed some damning evidence against the state's case, including some procedural irregularities, but they would never hear from him. Next, his execution date was scheduled." It would be a matter of days away if not commuted by the governor.

"You really need to be there as support for Trevon," the warden Arber told me. I supported a retrial to throw out the death penalty in his case, but the women's movement pushed back hard. "They have a lot of power in this city." Warden Arber answered.

I said I would be there, and then arranged to drive to the prison but couldn't find a sitter. So I had to take Angela with me. She could wait in the visitors' area and I assumed she didn't know about the purpose of the visit. It turns out she was more aware than we had suspected.

On the way, I ran out of gas! What a time to have this problem. I wanted to be there to pay my last respects to Trevon and say goodbye and thank him for being such a good father to our daughter, and also for his kindness to me. Fortunately, a policeman driving by me saw my car on the side of the road, turned around, and pulled in behind me, I assumed to help. When he walked to my car, he asked me where I was going.

"To the state prison to see the father of my daughter." The policeman then looked at Angela sitting in the back seat and it appeared that something clicked.

He said, "Oh, I see," and said he had a gas can in his patrol car. He ran back to fetch it, and put a gallon or so in my tank.

"I always have a safety can filled with gas for situations just like this," he told me as he put the gas in my tank.

"How much do I owe you?" I asked.

"Nothing," he answered.

"You don't owe me anything. This is a gift for my niece." I had no idea what he was referring to. Maybe he had a favorite niece he had promised something to. Then I saw his police ID which said

Reginald Turner. It dawned on me. He must be Trevon's brother! Later I learned everyone called him Reggie, so I did as well.

He waited until I was able to start my car and said, "I will turn on my siren and you just follow me." We raced to the prison, his siren blaring. When we arrived, I parked and followed him into the prison. He was obviously a very in command take-charge person.

We were led to the execution chamber just in time to see Trevon walk past the execution visitors' window.

At that moment Angela somehow realized what was happening, and screamed frantically, almost hysterically, "Please don't kill my Daddy! Don't kill my father! Don't you kill my Daddy!"

The guard then yelled, "What is she doing here! Children aren't allowed in here to witness an execution!"

Then, in the chaos, the guards grabbed her and she strenuously resisted their attempts to remove her, yelling, screaming and aggressively kicking the guards attempting to remove her. I attempted to calm her, without success. When she was finally out of the secure area, a friend of Warden Arber drove her to our pastor's home. I thought that was a good idea because she liked our pastor's wife who taught the children's Sunday school at church.

All this was observed by Trevon. He was furious, yelling, "Why did you let my daughter in here! That was cruel, inhumane, terribly wrong! What were you fools thinking!"

Warden Arber was called and he was also very angry at this turn of events.

"I run this place, or try to, and this is the worst incident that has occurred since I became warden. All of you know, I'm strongly opposed to this farce! I will call the governor again. He is the only one that can stop this tragedy. You all know my feelings. I have no authority to commute this sentence to life in prison which I have supported for over a year now!"

In the meantime, Trevon was returned to his cell to wait for the governor's response.

The media covering the demonstration picked up the news and carried the story, causing radio reports to broadcast the delay.

"You have another problem," the warden's aide noted.

"The crowd, mostly the local women's groups, are waiting for the execution of Trevon so they can celebrate. They now have word of the delay and are very angry, really angry!" the warden's aide relayed to us, obviously very upset at this turn of events.

Warden Arber then interviewed a few persons and learned how the mistake happened. The person responsible wasn't at his guard station when required. He was fired on the spot. Arber then called the governor and explained the situation.

After about twenty minutes, the warden announced that the execution wouldn't be delayed any longer. He then told me that the problem was the governor had to have the women's vote to be reelected, and they were fifty-six percent of the state's population. In this instance, letting a convicted rapist and murderer escape punishment could end his career. "We live in a democracy, you know. Voters rule!" he added.

He further noted, "The people rule, and the people in this case want Trevon to die."

The result was the prison delayed the execution for about an hour. Trevon was then taken from his cell and marched back to the execution room. Word got out of this turn of events and the crowd outside cheered, yelling, almost singing, "Justice for Susie Tompkins! Justice for Susie Tompkins" over and over.

Finally, Trevon made his final statement, speaking slowly and quietly but showing signs of being shaken up from the ordeal with his daughter and looking at the end of his days on Earth. He said, "I'm sorry, I really am. Thank you for forgiving me. I leave you all as I came—in love." Lastly, he asked for forgiveness and expressed his faith and the comfort he was given from his renewed Christian faith at this very difficult time in his life. After knowing him for almost a year, I have no doubt that he was sincere. On August 26, at 7:22 p.m., the 34-year-old father of our child was executed.

Several veteran witnesses of past executions remarked that he went to his death with a calmness and peacefulness that they had rarely ever seen before. His fourth court attorney, on his last call to me, said with some anger, "I see they fried another one without the required due process."

I was upset, angry, and heartbroken. "This event was almost as traumatic as when I was raped," I told Warden Arber.

We thought his daughter's outburst may have actually positively affirmed Trevon. He now knew that this little girl clearly loved him as a father. Knowledge of that fact was central to how he viewed himself. I had to wonder if his life would have been very different if he had experienced his daughter's love a decade ago.

Outside the prison, a crowd was celebrating, openly cheering his execution. When I tried to talk to them, explaining my daughter just lost her father, one demonstrator screamed at me.

"He was a despicable human, if you could call him that, a murderer and a rapist, one of the most terrible crimes imaginable, and we are happy his victim, Susie Tompkins, finally got the justice she deserved. He deserved to die for what he did. They should have torched him to death. Made him suffer as much as possible before that evil man died."

I answered, "You have just condoned the death of a loving father who had much to give the world and his family." That made them even more angry. The forty-five or so people, mostly women, were now openly livid with anger and proceeded to condemn me in the strongest words possible. I was thankful that Angela wasn't there to hear what they were saying, and I was enormously thankful that Reggie was there with me in his uniform. He said nothing but his commanding presence was most comforting.

Reggie enabled me to get into my car and drive home. When home, I locked the door behind me. I was frightened, so I also closed the shade. I felt someone was following me, but saw no evidence of this, even though I looked behind me several times. About twelve minutes later, a glass jar filled with some flammable liquid like gasoline with a burning rag connected to it crashed through my front living room window. It was a flaming Molotov cocktail! Someone across the street called the police and the fire department. No doubt attracted by all of the commotion, they were looking out of their windows when the firebomb was tossed through my window.

Reggie heard the police report on his police radio, and so knew it was my house that was hit. With the siren blaring, he raced to my house. Fearing the worst, he arrived in maybe five or six minutes. When he arrived I was just leaving to escape the fire, which was now raging. I had attempted to put it out and realized my attempt was futile. I got into his car and was whisked to the police station to make a report. The fire was soon put out, but not after major damage occurred to the home I had rented. I lost most everything in the front of the house, but later learned Angela had wisely hidden the wood carving of her in our car which we retrieved later! Did she know something we didn't?

After we made a report at the police station, Reggie drove us to his mother's house. He then called the station and had the department make sure no one followed the unmarked car that transported Angela and me to his mother's home.

We found out later that Warden Arber resigned as a result of the Trevon case, saying "One must always do what is right, and not what the crowd feels is right."

I also found out Pastor Anderson visited Trevon on the day of his execution and when asked about the visit he only said, "We are good, very good. It went very well."

CHAPTER 13

A New Home

In that one day, Angela and I had more than enough trauma to last a lifetime. Reggie drove me to assess the damage to our cottage home. When I saw it was not inhabitable, I told Reggie we needed to find a motel room or another place to stay. He said, "Nothing doing. My niece and you are going to stay at my mother's house."

I protested, but Reggie explained, "You are family, and I'm sorry, I don't know how White people behave in these situations, but when we have room, we don't behave by sending relatives to live in motels. That is insulting and we just don't do it. I will have the investigation crew gather your things up and have them brought to my mother's house."

To keep the peace, I acquiesced. I realized that, as strange as it sounded, this was my family now and I had better learn to accept that fact. Since my parents were deceased, this was my only family. We arrived back at their home, a sprawling brick home in a nice part of town. Next to his mother's home was a smaller house that, Reggie explained, was where he lived. Both homes, although probably sixty-or-more-years old, were immaculate: the yard, the home, and the neighborhood. The inside looked immaculate as well. The furnishings were a mixture of some relatively old, but well-maintained, and some newer, furniture that Reggie described as early attic.

"Most of the furniture was rebuilt or refinished quality walnut or oak style. Refinishing furniture is my hobby to help me relax," Reggie noted with an obvious sense of pride in his work.

He then added, "My father was a woodworker until he died, God bless his soul. He died when in his late twenty's, and Mom never remarried. My brother and I were only in grade school. Both of us loved working with wood," he explained.

Possibly to help me get my mind off of the traumatic day, he then added, "We would buy old furniture at the Goodwill for ten or twenty dollars. Often the furniture had several coats of paint, which we would strip and carefully refinish. It often looked like new or better, when we were done."

As I looked around, I noted the furniture was beautifully refinished, as was the rest of the living room. Reggie then called Pastor Anderson to retrieve Angela. When the pastor's wife answered, Reggie explained all that had happened and gave her directions to his mother's house.

About this time Reggie's mother, Martha, an attractive, slim woman of about sixty, came out of their wood-lined library and, as soon as she saw us, said, "I'm so very glad to meet you and am looking forward to meeting my granddaughter!"

Martha then looked at me and said, "I guess that would make you my daughter-in-law."

I motioned to Reggie to come closer and whispered the fact that Trevon and I were not married. Angela was her granddaughter, but I wasn't her daughter-in-law.

"We were not married," I added out loud.

To which Martha responded, "As far as I'm concerned, you are my daughter-in-law. End of story." She said it with a warm smile that showed her glistening white teeth. Still shaking, I was in no mood to argue with her, so chose to ignore the details. You couldn't help but like her, and I warmed up to her very quickly.

Maybe my life will improve now. No more trauma or drama. Martha was a sweet woman, I thought to myself, hoping my life and that of my daughter's would settle down.

About that time the pastor's wife arrived with Angela. When she was in the house, I introduced her to her grandmother and Reginald. Angela looked puzzled, so I explained our home was damaged and that we would be staying in her grandmother's house for a few days.

Martha then grabbed Angela and gave her a big hug! Then she said in her kind, but firm, voice, "I'm so glad to see you!" Your father had so much good to say about you! I have your pictures and had copies made to display in my pride corner," she said as she pointed to the wall where the family pictures were located. We then explained to Angela that Martha was her father's mother, so she was her grandmother. "Martha is the mother of your father, so she is, in a way, my mother-in-law."

Martha then began fussing about Angela, asking her if she was hungry.

"Yes, I am. I'm very hungry," she replied mixed up about the strange turn of events, and the two proceeded to the kitchen with Martha holding her hand. I was worried about her traumatic experiences of the day and just held my breath, hoping the diversion would help her get through the night and the weeks ahead. Home would have been comforting, but going back wasn't possible now. It wasn't habitable, and, as I didn't own the little cottage but was only a renter, I had no idea when that responsibility would be taken care of. I just knew we would again have to look for another place to live . . . and soon.

Martha then stepped in, adding, referring to Angela, "Now that I have met you, I can begin to spoil you! It is so wonderful to meet you," she said, as she gave Angela another big hug. Angela loved the attention and it helped distract her when dealing with the loss of her father.

The warm reception at the Turner's home somewhat dimmed the loss of our home which was still traumatic. In one day, Angela lost her father and our home was firebombed, yet, as it turned out, Angela met her grandmother who turned out to be a godsend, a wonderful loving person. And she managed to spoil Angela . . . to both of their pleasures!

Then Reggie stepped in and explained, "I can think of no better place for you to stay than here. Grandma can watch Angela while you are at work, and we have a large four-bedroom home here. You can have one room, Angela the other. You must realize family is very close to our hearts in our culture, especially grandmothers. In view of what Angela went through, I don't think pushing her onto a new babysitter in a strange home is a good idea. She has someone, a blood relative, here who loves her and will be with her all day."

I then voiced my approval, adding, "In view of the trauma, I agree. The firebomb nearly hit me, and what happened to my daughter's father today must have been the most traumatic day in her life. Hopefully this will be the worst day that will visit her, ever. I think she is somewhat numb now and the full impact of what she saw may hit her later."

I felt thankful that Reggie stepped in to help. I already had a good feeling about him. He had done so much for us already. After all he was a blood relative, so I should feel this way.

Soon afterwards, Reggie drove his truck and a neighbor came with him to help pick up a few necessary things from our burnt-out home until the rest was returned to us. As a policeman, he could walk past the police tape that said "CRIME SCENE— KEEP OUT!" It turned out most of the few things we had were in the bedrooms, which were in the back of the cottage, and weren't damaged except for some smoke damage. So, they filled up the truck and hauled our things over to where we were now staying. We had separate bedrooms with Angela in the smaller one next to the master bedroom, which became my room. Grandma Martha was in the guest bedroom, where she had always slept since her husband died. She could no longer sleep in the room where she and her husband had slept.

Reggie lived in his own house next door. Strange, I thought. Is he a mama's boy? Angela slowly adjusted and Reggie took her to work with him when he had desk work to do, which, as the police chief, was often. and that helped her adjust. As always, she was the center of attention.

CHAPTER 14

Getting to Know My
New Relatives

The next morning, I went to work and felt that Angela was comfortable enough to stay with her grandmother. To be sure, I called her four or five times during the day. She explained that she and her grandmother had played some games, made lunch, took a walk, and then went to the store to fulfill her grandmother's promise to spoil her. Martha bought her an entirely new outfit; it was very expensive and pink—just what she wanted and I could never afford.

Later that day, I found out Reggie had previously met with Trevon in the prison to make the required legal arrangements to bury his brother's body and deal with Trevon's worldly possessions, mostly his art work and carvings. When converted to money, all of his possessions amounted to several thousand dollars, all of which, I learned, was put in a trust fund for Angela. She could start withdrawing these funds beginning when she turned ten! I was given the authority to manage the money.

"I'm surprised and feel complimented," I told Reginald. I then added, "It appears that he really thought highly of both his daughter and me."

I learned later that most of the money came from the sale of his art which was managed by an art studio in New York. The funds weren't sent back to the prison to avoid the problem of earning money for the work he did there. Rather, they were all put in a trust fund, which was later put in Angela's name.

Reggie remarked, "He was clearly thinking of you and his daughter when he was gone. This was an attempt to be responsible about his obligation to care for his family." I was amazed! A major complaint of so many of my friends was their irresponsible husbands and ex-husbands who put themselves first and fiercely neglected their basic family responsibilities. Trevon clearly wasn't one of these kinds of fathers.

In the end, I agreed to pay rent for staying there. I could afford it and, I learned from Reggie, that Martha badly needed the money. Her social security check no longer covered all of the bills as it once did. Reggie also had to help her out.

We decided to put Angela in preschool again to give her grandmother some time for herself. On one of my days off Reggie and I sat down to talk. I was very careful to not sound too nosey but I was curious about him. He was a very handsome soft spoken man.

About this time I received a letter from William Kline, the distant cousin whose father put me through nursing school, an act of kindness for which I will always be grateful. They've always been very helpful to family, even to somewhat distant relatives as we were. Billy related his father, David, had died and he sent me information about the funeral. This news saddened me. He was so young and helped so many persons. In response to his letter, I wrote a long letter to Billy, expressing my appreciation for all he did for me.

CHAPTER 15

Settling in to a Routine

With me at work, Angela in day school, and Reggie still a full time police officer, we had some regularity in our lives. Grandmother usually fixed dinner and I was promoted at the hospital to a charge nurse, so I now had more regular hours. Reggie already had enough seniority to work from 9:00 to 5:00, so we all ate together every night. One day, I asked how his day went.

"Oh, pretty ordinary. Just the usual, catching the bad guys and then having the probation department let them go. I did have an unexpected event happen, though."

"Please tell us about it!"

"We got a domestic abuse call. Their young son actually called it in. So off we went."

"And?"

"When we got to the house we could hear screaming and loud arguing. We knocked on the door, rang the bell . . . and heard nothing. Afraid that this domestic violence call may end up a homicide, we broke the door down and saw a large burly man that must have weighed two-hundred pounds, who had his hands around what we assumed was his wife's neck. She was no small chicken either."

"And?"

"I grabbed the man and my partner attempted to get the wife away from the man. Then, in seconds, the wife began beating on me, kicking me while screaming, 'You leave my husband alone!'"

Surprised, I responded, "That just doesn't make sense!"

"Police officers know one of the most dangerous calls in our work are domestic abuse situations, so we expected it, but not to the degree that we encountered in this case."

"Are you alright?" I asked.

"We called for backup and within ten minutes the support team was there, but the wife had kicked me so many times that I had to go to the hospital and have an x-ray."

"Oh, dear!" I screamed.

"No broken bones, just a lot of bruises. A lot of bruises!"

"And?"

"I was put on a very strong dose of analgesics, and then went back to the station to fill out the police report on the event."

"Oh, you poor dear!" I said, feeling sorry for him. I was thankful that he wasn't hurt worse than he was.

"I want to go to bed as soon as we finish dinner," Reggie added, obviously sedated somewhat.

"Please do! I will do your job of cleaning up the kitchen and doing the dishes."

"Thanks! I will owe you a big favor," he added, before he went next door to hit the sack.

I was now spending a lot of time with Reggie, actually the three of us often did things together. He was great with Angela and they had bonded extremely well. His attention helped Angela adjust. We were almost a family, at least that is what I thought. When we went places, people saw us as an interracial couple with a light brown child, me the mother, and Reggie the father.

As we got to know each other, I could not help but wonder, was I good enough for this stiff upper lip perfectionist? After a few months I thought we needed to talk about us, and our future, if there was a future. These thoughts of mine surprised me, and I felt a little guilty about them. I got along very well with Reggie, but we both had a lot of baggage, at least I thought we did. Or, at least *I* did.

CHAPTER 16

Meeting with a Therapist

I made an appointment with a psychologist, Dr. Tom Walker, who worked with rape victims about the remaining issues that bothered me about Trevon.

"Could you help me understand why a man would rape a woman? Why not just wine and dine attractive women, and then become romantically involved? Trevon was a fairly good-looking man and he had a nice personality to boot!" I explained.

"Good question, one that I'm often asked by persons who were raped, as well as the parents and the families of persons convicted of rape. It is complex, the many factors involved are somewhat nebulous, but, in my experience, loss of the father, by death when the boy is very young, is often involved."

"Yes, I had heard that. I think that was true in Trevon's case," I added. He continued: "Another factor I have found in common is poor self-confidence and a strong fear of rejection, often a result of being rejected when young. This can be traumatic to a sensitive male, which is true of many, or at least some, males, who progress to become rapists."

"And?" I asked, intrigued by his insight.

"Thus, forcing the female to submit puts him in full control."

"That's for sure! And a gun sure helps!" I added.

"He feels power in the rape situation which helps to compensate for his inferiority complex. And with the gun, he has enormous power and the woman feels fear, for logical reasons."

"That's very true. I felt absolutely terrified then as would any woman."

"Very true. He isn't all powerful, but is in absolute command in that situation. Holding a gun, especially a handgun, makes most all people feel super powerful."

"In my case, Trevon had a handgun which he held onto even when he had completely overpowered me. He couldn't let go of that gun no matter what. He clung to it like it was a child's security blanket. It ended up killing someone, and he paid for his security blanket with his life," I added.

Dr. Tom added, "I need to stress that other factors are involved in rape, such as aggression, bad experiences with females, and especially early sexual experiences. Often when males are raped or molested by another male, it leads the victim into homosexuality. Studies have consistently found about 80 percent of priest molestations involve male priests and teenage boys," he added.

I now had a much better handle on this problem. I still had a lot of questions, but I guess in the end I will never fully understand it. Human behavior is ever so complex! It just helps a lot to talk about it with someone who understands the behavior and that's why I went to him.

I wish life was simple, but it isn't. I still have a lot of mixed emotions about my experience with Trevon.

CHAPTER 17
A Talk with Grandmother

Tell me about your son Reginald, I mean Reggie. He seems like a very nice man."

"Oh, he is that all right. He is a perfectionist. He once got a B in high school and couldn't sleep that night. He consistently got ones, the highest mark possible for citizenship. One time he got a two for less-than perfect behavior. All the rest were ones, but he was very upset. His brother rarely got twos, usually threes or fours, and I felt 'couldn't my two sons be more balanced?' They really took the loss of their father hard, especially Reggie, but they responded in very different ways to the loss. Reggie felt the loss was his fault and became a perfect boy in response. In my opinion, he became a little too perfect, perfect with everything, his room, his dress, everything," she added.

"He isn't perfect. The Bible says no one is perfect."

"True, but he tried to be perfect in human terms," Martha added, looking a tad downcast.

After pausing, she added, "His brother was the opposite. He became an irresponsible lazy slob in everything he did. He flunked out of school, life and work. He would work odd jobs and rarely stayed on a job for more than a month or two, then quit and who knows what he did. Evidently, he stalked women, with the goal of raping them. Especially women who had the same work schedule each day. Once he knew their schedule, he would lie in wait for them to arrive home from work to attack them. The lawyer told me it could take him months to find a woman who was alone at night in areas where few people frequented."

"That described my situation perfectly!! I see I was in line for trouble," I remarked.

"I'm glad I moved out of my apartment when I did," I added, now having a better understanding of what happened and why.

Although I felt she was a typical mother complaining about her son, I knew she loved Trevon and was devastated by what happened in the end. This is why she didn't attend his execution. I was surprised that Reggie could. I don't blame her for not attending. What mother wouldn't have a difficult time with what happened?

Martha continued, "And the therapist who tried to help us deal with the loss added that the fatherless generation, those who lost their fathers as my boys did, had special problems. He helped me deal with my sons. Let me show you the information he gave me."

With that she opened a drawer and retrieved a one page sheet. She gave me the sheet and this is what it said:

> 80% of rapists with anger problems come from fatherless homes, fully 14 times the average. (Data from *Justice & Behavior*, Vol. 14, pp. 403-426)

> 90% of all homeless and runaway children are from fatherless homes, 32 times the average level.

> 85% of all children who show behavior disorders come from fatherless homes, 20 times the average level. (From *The Centers for Disease Control Data*)

71% of all high school dropouts come from fatherless homes, 9 times the average rate. (Data from *National Principals Association Report*)

70% of youths in state-operated institutions come from fatherless homes, also 9 times the average. (Data from *U.S. Dept. of Justice*)

85% of all youths in prison come from fatherless homes, 20 times the average. (Fulton Co. Georgia, Texas Dept. of Correction)

After reading this list, I commented, "I can see how Trevon's loss of his father could have had a devastating influence on him."

"Yes, but the therapist cautioned that a lot of other factors could have influenced him, and people aren't numbers; every person is unique."

She then interrupted my train of thought, adding about Reggie, "When he cleaned his room he would take everything out of his room, including his bed, and clean everything as he put his things back. He would clean out his drawers, dust them, and put everything back in order." As she covered these traits of her son, I realized she was describing me! I did the same things. My house was as perfect as I could get it. I cleaned whether it needed it or not!

"What about girlfriends?" I then asked his mom.

"No one was ever good enough for him. I felt if he got a girlfriend she would have to be a little aggressive or Reggie would be single for the rest of his life. He was also a prude. I told him, 'Be affectionate and act normal.' Maybe he will get to like some girl. He said he will be a virgin when he marries, if he ever does, which I kind of doubt now."

I thought that was me as well! Reggie was exceptionally nice and polite to me, but showed no romantic interest in me, none. He was a perfect gentleman. I had the strong feeling that Martha would like Reggie to get married for a lot of reasons. She wanted a grandson. I have to admit I was intrigued with him, but felt marrying what my new family called my brother-in-law, would be a very bad idea. Nonetheless, Martha was very open with me, and I appreciated that. She loved both her sons, but I felt she was at times somewhat critical of both of them. I guess this was true of most mothers. I couldn't help feeling she thought I was perfect for Reggie. It was just a feeling, and nothing that she ever said.

The next week I had an appointment with my pastor to fill him in on my life and thank him again for his help in deciding what to do about my pregnancy problem.

CHAPTER 18

Another Meeting with Pastor Anderson

"H i, pastor," I said as soon as I saw him.

After I explained the concern about my mixed feelings toward my brother-in-law, he said, "You know in the Bible when the father of a child died, the father's brother was obligated to marry his dead brother's wife and rear his child. The concern in the Scriptures is the child, and the child first. Another example was, if a man died and didn't have a son, the brother-in-law had an obligation to marry his widow and father a son."

"What? That sounds immoral, to say the least," I shot back in amazement.

"I'm referring to the story of Onan." He then took out his well-thumbed Bible, and in his favorite translation, read Genesis 38:8-10 which said the widow "of her deceased brother in the event his brother had produced no male heir."

Pastor Anderson mentioned to help me understand the passage. He continued reading from Genesis 38:6-10

> "Now Judah acquired a wife for Er, his firstborn, and her name was Tamar. But Er, Judah's firstborn, was wicked in the LORD's sight;

so the LORD put him to death. Then Judah said to Onan, "Sleep with your brother's wife. Perform your duty as her brother-in-law and raise up offspring for your brother. But Onan knew that the offspring would not belong to him; so whenever he would sleep with his brother's wife, he would spill his seed on the ground so that he would not produce offspring for his brother. What he did was evil in the sight of the LORD."

"But that is Old Testament and part of the Jewish law. We as Christians aren't under Jewish law today," I protested.

"Right you are! I always respected you because you are intellectually sharp and knowledgeable."

I smiled at the compliment and said nothing. Pastor Anderson continued, "The New Testament at Matthew 22:24 includes the same teaching. He then read: "If a man dies without having children, his brother is to marry the widow and raise up offspring for him."

Thus, Pastor Anderson continued, "It is clear that if a man dies, his brother shall marry his wife and raise up the seed of his brother. These scriptures don't even hint that for a widow to marry her brother-in-law is problematic. In fact, it seems the right thing to do in some cases. I realize this is not exactly your situation, but there is a parallel. Are you engaged to Reggie?"

"No, I'm not."

"Has he proposed?"

"No, he hasn't."

"Have you dated?"

"No, I just get good vibes from him."

"It could be he is just a kind, considerate man to everyone he meets."

"Well, that could well be. He certainly is that!"

"OK, it doesn't hurt to think ahead." Pastor Anderson added.

"True, and I'm trying to do that now. That is why I'm asking you these questions."

"I see. That is a good idea." Pastor Anderson answered. "You might let him know how you feel."

"I don't think I could do that." "Why?"

"I'm not a forward kind of woman, and neither is he a forward kind of man."

"Well someone has to take the first step and it may have to be you."

After thinking for a few seconds, I blurted out, "I was afraid you would say that."

"Well, just keep being kind to him. One never knows!" Pastor Anderson answered with a warm smile on his face. He smiled a lot.

"I agree. And I want to thank you for the help. In my case at least, you have always been right!"

"Thanks for the compliment, but I do have a fair share of skeletons in my own closet, as do most people. Nevertheless, I sure appreciate the compliment!"

Before I left, Pastor Anderson read another scripture to me, Matthew 6:14-15 from the Amplified Version:

> For if you forgive others their trespasses [their reckless and willful sins], your heavenly Father will also forgive you. But if you do not forgive others [nurturing your hurt and anger with the result that it interferes with your relationship with God], then your Father will not forgive your trespasses.

He then added "I'm reading this to you because, from this scripture, it seems to me, judging from our conversations in the past and today, that you have forgiven Trevon and God has forgiven you of your trespasses. Think about this."

"I will," I responded as I thanked him again for his advice.

"One more thing. I have worked with people in my church who told me of horrible things that happened in their lives. They usually explained their situation with visible anger, which I could understand, but then I learned the event they were discussing with me occurred over a half century ago! They just couldn't let it go and move on. This resentment then built up, and they became angry, bitter persons that no one wants to be around for good reason."

"I too have known such people," I added "so I fully understand what you are saying." I again thanked him and left, looking forward to my future and the goodness I was confident was now in store for me.

CHAPTER 19
The Turner Household

T hings were going very well at the Turner household. I was able to focus on my position at the hospital and Angela was adjusting as well as could be expected. Her grandmother and Reggie both were very active in her life. Reggie was like a father, very attentive, always doing things with Angela, and she loved his attention. At times I was jealous! But, very proud of my little angel.

In the evening, we had talks about our daily events, our concerns, and especially our past. I avoided talking about the trauma the rape caused, partly because it was a sensitive subject for both myself and the Turners. One day, however, the topic of Trevon was broached.

Martha piped in with, "He was always a difficult child compared to his brother. As I look back on his childhood, he really missed his father. When his dad passed away, everything became worse, especially between him and his brother."

She then added, repeating what she related to me before, that "Trevon became aggressive and angry at the world. Reggie kept it all in and became a perfectionist and an over-achiever to prove to his father that he loved him and deserved his love."

"Why was Trevon so difficult as a child, and so different than his brother?" I asked, wondering.

"I have to admit that we gave Reggie more positive attention. He was just a more easygoing, and a more pleasant child in spite of the fact that he was too much of a perfectionist."

"Was there any other event where Trevon felt rejected?" I asked.

"I really cannot think of any. Maybe he just *felt* more. He was a very sensitive child and may have felt rejected even though he wasn't. From my observation, Trevon was a lot more aggressive in certain areas than his brother."

"Was there nothing specific that you remember caused him to feel more rejected?"

"There was one incident, when he was in eighth grade, involving a girl he liked a lot who sat behind him. Trevon accidently knocked her books off of her desk and onto the floor. He felt embarrassed and picked them up for her. Looking for a compliment after he picked her books up, he didn't get one. Instead, she berated him for being clumsy and knocking her books off her desk. She then put her books back on the school room floor. But I can't think that that one example was all that important. He did tell me about it, so it must have been important to him. He was rejected again, and it seems this experience bothered him more than it should."

"But could there have been many similar events like that which he didn't tell you about?"

"Of course. As he got older, he didn't confide in me as much as when he did when he was younger, at least it appeared that he didn't. I guess we will never know all that went through Trevon's mind that caused him to be the way he was. Part of the reason was he never liked to go to church, but Reggie did, or at least he didn't complain as much about going. I wish I had a chance to talk to him before he was executed, but I really had a difficult time going to the prison to talk to him. I strongly felt he wouldn't be executed. He had such glowing reports in the prison for his behavior, especially after he got to know his daughter. When the date was announced I didn't take it seriously, but I'm sure the pressure from the women's movement had something to do with his execution. I'm not much of a women's libber."

She then added, "I had two sons, a great husband, a wonderful father, two very protective brothers, and some great nephews, so I have always, well, almost always, had good relationships with men. I have to wonder if women libbers aren't just angry at men because of bad relationships with them, possibly due to their own difficult personality."

I responded to this revelation about women's lib with, "I have had a few bad relationships with men, so can understand the feelings of some women. I'm sure glad I didn't marry Robert!"

I then switched the conversation back to Trevon, and Martha exclaimed, "When I asked the prison therapist about Trevon, she had some insight, but in the end she said we will never know for sure. "Humans are far too complicated for us to understand these things," she remarked. "Someone else in his shoes would have never taken the road to cause so much pain and suffering as Trevon did," she added as some reassurance to his mother's thoughts.

CHAPTER 20
Dinner at Reggie's House

One day, out of the blue, Reggie asked me over to his house for dinner. "Would you like to come over this evening for dinner?" he asked.

"I would love to," I replied, with a very happy smile on my face. When 6:00 pm came, I was there right on time. I was shocked. It was a candle-lit dinner with all of the trimmings; filet mignon, a salad and pecan pie, all my favorites.

"How did you know all of my favorite dishes?" I asked, not really knowing how he knew.

"Angela told me!"

"She did?"

"Yes. That little girl knows more than you or I will ever know!"

"I'm sure you are right!" I answered, realizing now that they spend a lot of time together, my interest in food and other things likely came up.

As I was being served by my charming host, I looked around his house. Clean, tastefully decorated and everything in its place. Besides that, it had numerous pictures of his family. I looked for Trevon's picture but it was nowhere to be found. Maybe I just couldn't recognize his picture, so I asked him.

"Where is Trevon's picture?"

"He was the problem child in the family so he wasn't included in my selection. He caused the family endless, enormous embarrassment. One uncle was a doctor, my great grandmother was a lawyer, a barrister, when Jim Crow laws were at their height, so we have a very proud family history. I have uncles that became policemen, one even became the mayor of a small, largely white town out West. We also had more than our fair share of preachers and ministers. One even pastored a largely white congregation. And no small number were musicians, actually many were, who played jazz music in New Orleans. None that I know of had an arrest record. Not one."

"I see, you do have a very illustrious family history."

"So you understand, as you would expect, the family response to Trevon was very negative, and I don't blame them. It reflects poorly on my mother, me and the entire family. And we have a large extended family."

We then, thankfully, got off on to discussing other things. I apologized mentioning "I probably shouldn't have brought Trevon up, but I was curious."

Reggie added, "Did you know Angela thought her father was executed for what he did to you!"

"You're kidding! Why would she think that?"

"We talked a lot about her life, her dad, the courts, prisons, and many other topics. I hate to mention this but it appears to me that she confides more in me than you. It must be the father-daughter thing."

"No, I'm glad she has a good relationship with you. Very glad. Just like I had with my father. He was a wonderful man and I was very blessed for the years I spent with him."

Before we began eating, Reggie grabbed my hand and said the prayer. He had become very active in his local Baptist church and expressed his faith, rarely in words, but commonly in deeds. I have to admit I liked his quiet, but effective, way of manifesting his inner convictions. This was also the first time he held my hand.

I felt it was comforting. As his mother said, the only way he will ever marry is if the woman was a little forward. To be forward was not me, though I guess he may be single for quite a while.

As the evening came to an end, I had to admit to myself that I had a memorable evening, and was very happy with how well I got along with Reggie. When I noticed it was after 10:00, I said that I had to go back to my room next door.

Before I left I asked why his mother named him Reggie.

"After Reginald Hawkins, the civil rights activist in Charlotte, North Carolina. I knew of him when I lived in North Carolina. He was the first African-American to run for Governor of North Carolina and fought to desegregate Charlotte schools and businesses. My father always admired him and he was a local African-American hero."

Reggie then politely said out of the blue, "I really enjoyed your company. Let's do this again sometime."

"Yes, I really would like to do this again. Next time, I would be honored to make the meal."

With that, we shook hands and I left. As I went back to my room, I was a very happy woman. I really enjoyed the evening. I had to admit it was the most romantic meal I have had in my 26 years of life! Reggie sure knew how to impress a girl! After a stunning evening, I was in bed by 10:30, ready to get some rest for my next long day at the hospital.

CHAPTER 21

Back Home

The next morning Martha asked, "How did it go?" "Wonderfully," I answered. "Much better than I expected. He was a perfect gentleman."

"It looks like my son finally found the perfect girl!"

"What do you mean?" I asked, not thinking about what she said earlier.

"Every girl he met didn't have this or that quality. She was either not very smart or too smart, too shy or too forward, too tall or too short, too skinny or too fat. I asked over and over and over what about Sandra Walter? I thought she was perfect. Or Malinda Gordon? He always found something wrong, always. I got tired of friends asking if he was gay, or what his problem was. Why he wasn't married."

I said nothing, just thought about what she said and thought it's about time I broke my mold and became a little forward. Just a little.

After that first formal meal, we dated. He was consistently a perfect gentleman. Considerate and polite to a fault

While dating, we met for dinner once or twice a week. We alternated on who cooked the meal. Either the meal I cooked was at grandmother's home where I stayed, or the meal he cooked was at his house. Soon we were cooking all of the meals at his home. To prepare for the meals, we went shopping together. It was clear we both enjoyed each other's company.

One day I sat down with him and said, "We need to talk about us and where this relationship is going."

"Where what is going?" he asked naively. "You and me."

"Us?" He was so take-charge as a policeman, yet he behaved like a teenager when it came to boy-girl relationships.

"I have a wonderful child, a great job, and have the same needs all women have for a loving husband."

I realized what his mother said was true. I would have to ask this tall, strapping 200-pound man about these sensitive areas. He was incredibly shy. Very different than when I met him on the way to the prison. He was then clearly a take-charge man and told me in no uncertain terms what to do. He was a perfect father and accepted me in spite of what happened. Not like Robert, who abandoned me during the most difficult part of my life. I never understood why, and he never told me why. Reggie unabashedly and consistently stood by me.

Finally, I stated, "We are just about married now. We see each other almost every day. Eat dinner together just about every night." He agreed and, to my surprise, said that was true and marriage would be a very good idea. It finally dawned on him about what I was driving at.

"A very good idea?" I thought to myself. Where was the enthusiasm? Why not come over to me and give me a big hug in response?

A few weeks later, formal and proper as always, he put a pillow on the living room floor, got on his knees, and formally proposed, pulling out the ring which he added was, "Just a loaner as I wanted you to choose the ring so you can have the one that you like best." I then saw him tear up; the first time I saw this emotional response! This meant more to me than the ring, more than the great dinners, although they were great, and very romantic. I just had to accept him as he was, and I did.

That Saturday, we were in the most exclusive jewelry store in the city, the *Blue Nile Diamond Jewelry* downtown, looking at rings. When I asked about a price range, he said, "The concern is you need to pick out what you like; it's not about the cost." So I did, but I didn't want anything too ostentatious, and it had to be petite. I also didn't want to take advantage of him.

The first person we wanted to tell about our marriage plans was, of course, Angela. That night we sat down with her to explain our plans.

"Angela," I said, "we have something to tell you."

"Yes, I'm all ears." I don't know where she picked that expression up, but she was very sensitive to words, and that was one reason why she was ahead of her peers in awareness. I thought she would make a good writer someday.

"Yes, mother?" She answered.

"Your uncle and I are getting married."

She looked at us with her eyes wide open and said nothing.

"Well, what do you think about our plans?" I added to break the spell.

"Is that legal?" she asked.

"Yes, legal and Pastor Anderson said it was scriptural as well."

"I thought relatives couldn't marry?" Angela asked with a puzzled look written all over her face.

I broke the spell answering, "Close blood relatives like brother and sister can't."

"Brother and sister! Who would want to marry their brother! That's really dumb," she added, no doubt thinking about her girlfriend's brothers.

"Well, what do you think about your uncle and me marrying?"

She answered the question, not by words, but by giving me and Reggie a big hug. That said a lot!

"Now the only issue is what do you call Reggie?" I asked Angela. She sat there thinking and said nothing for several minutes.

"Well, what do you want to call Reggie?" I asked again to get her thoughts.

"I don't want to call him dad because he isn't my real dad. Well, maybe I will call him 'Dad' and then call my real dad, 'my real dad'!"

"That will work fine for us. We want you to be happy with using whatever words that you choose. Our concern is that you are comfortable with the term you use. If you are happy with 'Dad', we are as well."

And so those were the terms Angela used to call her two fathers for as long as we can remember. As she grew older, we tried to help her understand her biological father, and what he did, and why. It was very difficult, but she saw her father as two different people. The good man she knew and loved replaced the bad man she never knew. His father was like a sick man who got well.

CHAPTER 22

The Wedding

W e were married at his Baptist church. It was packed. His minister gave a fiery sermon that bored no one. All of my friends came, as did many of my coworkers from the hospital, including Reggie's fellow officers. Dr. Rivera, the psychiatrist, and his wife, Mindy, were there as was Warden Arber. Even the mayor showed up, for the good food he said with a smile on his face. And of course Billy Kline was there. I noticed he had grown a lot since I saw him last. I almost didn't recognize him! He was now a handsome young man like his father.

Angela was glowing the whole time and got more attention than me. At least that's what it appeared to me, but I was proud, very proud, of her. She had brought so many blessings to me and so many others.

"I'm a lucky girl!" she told me at the wedding. I now have another father, so I have two fathers, my real dad and my other dad. I wish my real dad could be here," she added with more than a tinge of sadness.

"I also wish he was here." And I really meant it. I finally came to full forgiveness for what he did to me, as Pastor Anderson stressed I must.

I noticed all the 'races' got along great. I observed no friction. At the wedding of a white woman and an African American man, no one seemed to show any concern except a few African-American women who complained that they lost another good catch to a white woman.

"What's wrong with us," one asked. "The white gals are getting all of the good, eligible Black guys."

After the wedding, Angela and I moved into Reginald's house. It already had a bedroom and private bathroom ready for Angela. In the basement was Reggie's woodworking shop. Martha was thrilled. She continued to take an active role in the family. She said that was her culture. That's what many African American women she knew did; family was first, always first. She tried very hard to conscientiously treat everyone equally and I think she was very close in achieving her goal.

Then, in a little over a year, there was another addition to our family, a boy we named Stephen. Martha and my husband were ecstatic, so was Angela. She really wanted a brother, and now she had one to boss around. As the older sister, she was very protective of her brother. We had to add an addition onto the home to hold the entire happy family.

We now had the normal things to concern ourselves with: school, a few broken bones from sports, and the normal childhood sicknesses. Life was very good . . . finally.

I was truly blessed and told Pastor Anderson that his advice was wise and correct. I wondered if I had aborted Angela how things would have turned out. I realized some women who kept their baby didn't experience the same blessings I did. I have a hard time concluding that God hasn't blessed me for my stand in spite of the opposition from my peers and friends. I could only tell my story and pray that others could benefit from it. And this I have done as honestly as I could in this manuscript.

CHAPTER 23

An Interview at the Cemetery

That's our story," we told the writer, William Bucknell, who was interviewing us for his next book. "We all honor Trevon every year on his birthday by visiting the cemetery where he is buried. We celebrate how it was he, in an amazing turn of events, that created our family. I now have two wonderful children, a girl from Trevon, plus a boy from my 12-year marriage to his brother."

"How has your marriage worked out?" he asked.

"It's wonderful, simply wonderful; very much so. I just ran out of superlatives! I have a wonderful husband, more than any woman could ask for. Not once have I regretted marrying him," I said, while smiling at my husband who beamed back his appreciation.

"And your daughter?"

"Angela is now seventeen and working at a successful modeling career. She also has a steady boyfriend who she, and we, all adore."

"Great!" Mr. Bucknell said, as he again smiled.

"Her steady boyfriend is a white guy, a German actually, who was born in Germany, but she has dated some African-American guys. Race doesn't matter to her, as she can pass for white or black, this issue is irrelevant to her."

"She has the best of both worlds. She is a light-skinned black or a brown-skinned white, whichever fits the occasion," I added, beaming with pride about my daughter.

Asked if I would change anything in my past, I answered, "Actually, I would not change anything in my life, nothing, not even the worst day of my life. In the end, from the worst came the best, and I'm thankful for everything I have now."

I then added, "It was critical that I took to heart Pastor Anderson's words stressing forgiveness. I realized that if God could forgive Trevon, I certainly could. That advice helped me put my daughter's needs first, before my emotions, and to take the steps so that the two, my daughter and Trevon, could meet. This was the beginning of my confronting head-on the most horrible day of my life, and, at the same time, my daughter discovering her father. My life was finally put together. I'm so glad I did not marry Robert, or one of my other boyfriends!!"

Then Mr. Bucknell specifically asked Angela about her recollections about her father.

"I do remember the year with my Father was one of the happiest of my life. We spent about four hours a week together for almost a year and got to know each other quite well. He was a gift to me and I credit him for who I am today. His execution, though, I have never really gotten over. I have the games we played, and I tried to write down the jokes and other things we did. I have to remember the year with him was a gift that many little girls do not have.

Many do not even have as much time as I had with my father, so I'm fortunate, very blessed. It is better to have a year with a wonderful dad than a lifetime with an unloving father. I believe if he was not executed he would have done well and maybe even could have been released from prison. It is hard for me to justify his past, but everybody tells me he was a changed man. And I believe he was. I was told by more than one person, specifically including the warden, that his relationship with me was critical in the changes he made. The warden added that he has seen this change in a number of cases. I plan to do a book about him and my life now, and maybe become a writer like you. I have a lot of photographs that my grandmother kept, and I have spent much time looking at them with my grandmother. She told me so much good about him. All of us seem to have a dark side, some much darker than others, but most people also have a good side; Trevon certainly did.

"And any other plans for your future?" Mr. Bucknell asked.

"I have thought about going to law school to maybe fight some of the wrongs in our society. My real dad has inspired me. I learned so much from him. And I have a wonderful stepfather who I have called dad since my mother married him. I know half of my genes are from my actual father, and I guess about 25 percent of my genes are the same as my stepfather's. I also have a wonderful grandmother, so I am very blessed. I realize my blessings are what I have to focus on, not the evil, and I do, indeed, try very hard to focus on my many blessings."

Mr. Bucknell than asked, "I'm curious, and you do not need to answer if you feel uncomfortable, but, being a child of rape, what are your, well, thoughts?"

"I'm very glad to answer. My thoughts are my mother loved me so much that she went against the peer pressure to abort me. I realize I'm very fortunate to be alive, and because of this I relish even the small blessings in life. I also think I take some disappointments in life better than many people, at least as far as I can tell. I'm alive also, because my mother's acceptance of Christian teachings. If she was an atheist, or a nominal Christian, would I be here? I think not."

Mr. Bucknell then added, "You made a very good point about Christianity. I once heard Madalyn Murray O'Hair, the famous atheist, talk about her son who became a Christian, saying she would never talk to him again. When asked by a talk show host, 'What about forgiveness, after all, he is your son?' she answered, 'You Christians have to forgive your enemies. I'm an atheist and I do not have to forgive my son.' She never did talk to him, and when she was brutally murdered by two of her atheist employees for her money (she was by then a very wealthy woman), it was too late to change her mind. Thank you for the time you all have spent with me. I will send you a copy of the story when it is published."

"Thank you!"

"I want to add Angela is a member of an unusual group of offspring, children who were the product of rape, all by African American men who raped white women. There are only five of us but we all have done well. Three boys, and two girls, one now in his late twenties happily married.

I have another story, this one about our distant cousin, William David Kline, who has played an important role in my life. I learned much more about him when I heard the following report on the radio.

> *We have a witness of the accident. Tell us, what did you see?*
>
> *I saw a car over there (pointing to the viaduct)! It was traveling way too fast and barely made the turn onto the viaduct. It careened toward the guardrail and, unbelievably, rolled over the guardrail and plummeted hood-first down to the street which was about 40 feet below! Oh, it was horrible! The car landed head-on onto the pavement below with a loud crash. The noise was terrific and the car immediately burst into flames! I thought there was no way the driver or passenger, if there was one, could survive this. Not ever! This was terrible, the worst thing I have ever seen in my life! I then asked somebody to call 911!*
>
> *Soon the sirens were blaring to get to the accident, endeavoring to save anyone, . . . if by chance someone had survived. Another passerby said to the police*

stationed nearby, "As the car fell, I heard a child scream, "Help, Daddy! Help, me Daddy. Please help, Daddy!" When the car hit the pavement everyone in the car was killed."

I knew David Kline was now rich, smart and had a beautiful wife. But I would learn there was much more behind his story. But this is his story and I will let him tell it.

PART II
David's Story: Marrying Jezebel

"I have this against you: You tolerate that woman
Jezebel … By her teaching she misleads My servants
to be sexually immoral."

(Revelation 2:20. *Berean Study Bible*)

CHAPTER 1

Kindertransport

My name is William David Kline, the only child of Barbara and David Kline. My father, David, inherited a small business from his cousin. He built it up from a few employees to almost 200. This, though, is my story, not my father's. I have been called Billy since I could talk. My parents tell me as a child I could not say "William" but got out "Wilum." Since that's how I said my name, they just called me Billy.

Ever since then I have been known as Billy. I was William when my parents were angry at me, which was rare. I was a spoiled but sensitive child, bright but lazy, learning mostly by doing. This worked out well because, aside from school, I was with my dad working with him at his job as president of his company. My father lost most all of his family in Germany, including his parents, Rabbi Daniel Kline, who was born in Germany, and his wife, Marie Sara Blaine.

My father was one of the young children that was part of the Kindertransport (German for "children's transport"). Kindertransport was an organized rescue effort implemented shortly before the outbreak of the Second World War in 1939. Nearly 10,000 children, mostly Jewish from Nazi-occupied Austria, Czechoslovakia, Poland, and the Free City of Danzig, were sent to Britain. The children were placed anywhere there was a supportive home, including in British foster homes, hostels, schools, and even farms. The start of World War II brought the program to an end. As a result, millions of children died at the hands of the Nazis.

As was true of my family, often the Kindertransport children were the only members of their family that survived the Holocaust. Both my grandparents were murdered in the Holocaust. My father married my mother in London when they were both twenty-two. They then moved to the United States where I was born several years later. My father came to the United States to work for his cousin, and he eventually took over the business. This experience made my father what he is today. It also made him determined to give me the father that he never had. He made up for the lack of a father in his childhood by making sure his son, me, had a close relationship with him. And I did. Very close.

We worked together, played together and learned together. My world was my father and school. I did almost nothing with friends, except at school. I had no friends to speak of, aside from those I spent time with at school. Otherwise, I had a typical childhood, was an above-average student, and abnormally shy. This was partly because most of my time was not spent with the few friends I made in school, but with my parents and other adults, the persons who worked for, and with my father. I was thus in one way more mature than most of the kids I knew, but as I grew up largely in the adult world, I did not fit in with the school crowd very well. My story begins in high school, ninth grade to be exact, talking with my mom about my future, actually *our* future, my family and me.

CHAPTER 2

A Talk With Mom

When Dad was on a short business trip, mom told me we needed to have a talk. I was just entering high school and thought it was THE TALK about sex. We had learned more than enough about sex in school that I felt it was not likely she could add much more to what I already knew, or thought I knew.

"Sure, Mom. What's it about?" I asked, expecting THE TALK, and wondering why dad did not have this discussion with me instead of mom.

"It's about your father."

"My father? I was expecting THE TALK."

"No, not *the* talk; I want to talk about your father."

"Okay. I'm all ears."

"You need to know that your father was accidentally shot by a deer hunter several years ago. As a result, he has a damaged heart and is not expected to live a normal lifespan."

"What? Why didn't he tell me about this before?"

"For obvious reasons."

"Like what?"

"Like, he did not want you to worry. He is very protective of you."

"I just thought he was a great dad."

"He is that all right, but he is concerned about the business, the shop."

"What about the company?"

"He has worked his whole life building the company to what it is today. Working twelve to fourteen or more hours a day."

"I know that. I often worked with him."

"One reason he hired you to work was so he could spend as much time with you as possible."

"Yes, okay, I know—he keeps telling me that."

"He thinks the world of you and hopes that you will take over the leadership of the company when he dies. As I said, he does not have a normal life expectancy, and realizes each day he lives could be his last, so is grateful for everything and every day."

"Dad tells me the same thing almost every day!"

"I know, but with him he knows his time on Earth is limited. Along that line, he also has you work at the shop so you will know the business forward and backward, and then run it effectively when it is yours. Toward that goal, in high school you will need to take wood shop, metal shop, industrial drawing, auto shop, accounting, and all the business courses you can get."

"But what if I don't want to?" I objected.

"What classes do you want to take?" Mother asked.

"I want to take college preparatory classes, college English, physics, calculus. I am a straight-A student and want to go to college."

"You need to look at your future and how your father has prepared you to take over the family business."

Still independent, I fired back with, "It's my life. I can live it the way I want to!"

"True, but one other thing your father is concerned about is the effect of college on your spiritual life."

"What?" I was lost at this comment.

"You realize your father lost his bearing in college, as so many students have. He was bombarded with pessimism from some of his professors. One, an English professor, from the way he talked, seemed ready to commit suicide any day, and your father's roommate did commit suicide in his third year of college. Your father came home from class and found him dead. He shot himself in the head in their room."

"I never knew that."

"He felt much of college was a waste of time and that it did not prepare him for the real world. His philosophy class was the worst. It was in that class where he lost his faith in God and had to struggle for years to deal with the ideas of pessimism and negativity he learned there. As you know, his father was a rabbi, so he comes from a very devout family where religion was central to their life."

"Is that why he was always reading books on apologetics and creation and evolution?"

"Yes, that's partly why. He felt, as your professor uncle said, that the goal of professors is to make students as much unlike their parents as possible. He also had some great professors, especially in his pre-med courses."

"Pre-med? You mean he wanted to become a doctor?" This was the first time I heard this dream of dads.

"Yes, that was his goal. He was even accepted into a top medical school."

"What happened?"

"Me," mother answered.

"You?"

"Yes, it was not long after he met me that he wanted to get married. He was head over heels in love with me!"

"He still is. That's very obvious," I remarked.

"When we married, he was unable to get a job that could support me, so he came to America and your cousin hired him to work for his small shop which had twenty-eight employees at the time, and your father built it into its current close to five-hundred employees."

"I still think I want to live my own life," I added, thinking only of myself.

"No. It's your father's concern for you and your future. When we married we had to live with my parents and we struggled to survive. He does not want you to have the same experience."

"I'm not going to have to do that."

"You say that now, but you are not there yet. Your father was. Family is critical, as we found out, and you need to realize that fact. Your faith is critical as well."

Mother then added, "Things are a lot worse now in colleges Take a few classes at the local Christian college and live at home. There's no Hebrew university in our state, so at least at a Christian college you will not have Darwinism shoved down your throat as your dad experienced when he went to college. You need to think carefully about your future. If you work for your dad you will make a good living; you will not get rich, but it is an excellent company to work for. We have a high employee retention rate, impressively high."

"Actually, I want to thank you, Mom. I am sorry I was not very receptive at first, but I did not know all of these facts about father. I will have to think about what you said."

"That's all I want you to do. Love you, son."

"And I love you, mom. Always have, always will."

Well, that was the talk. I, though, did learn a few new things about my family.

CHAPTER 3

I Begin Tenth Grade

Well, I soon graduated from ninth grade and was ready to begin tenth grade. My best friend, Christopher, came up to me to let me know what was happening in his life. He was very different than me in personality and appearance. I was thin-built guy with jet black hair, light blue eyes, serious, quiet and studious. He was slightly heavy-set, black hair, brown eyes, very gregarious, fun-loving and had better things to do than read schoolbooks or study for exams. In spite of our differences we bonded from first grade and have been fast friends ever since.

When Christopher approached me, he asked, "Are you still working for your dad, Billy?"

"Yes, I work full-time in the summer and thirty hours a week during school, mostly on weekends."

"And full-time in the summer?" "Yes, I said that."

"You work a lot of hours. Is that legal? I am looking for a part-time job next year and have to get a work permit. And I cannot work more than twenty hours a week. The paperwork and rules are amazing, all for a silly job in some fast-food restaurant!"

"Well, I work for the family business, so we have a lot more leeway," I answered. "We have talked about this in the past, so I do not know why it's coming up again."

"I'm a little jealous, I guess," Christopher responded.

I think he wanted the benefits of work but did not want to work, now or in the future.

"I am saving up my money and plan to buy a new Corvette when I am sixteen," I added.

"A Corvette! No way. Look, I know your dad runs a big business, and he is the largest employer in town, but he is turning you into a spoiled rich kid."

"Not really. I have to earn every penny I need to pay for the car. My dad said if you work hard, you deserve a few nice things! After all, the Bible says a worker deserves his wages."

"Where does it say that."

At First Timothy 5:18 which says, "The worker is worthy of his wages."

"That's in the New Testament!"

"I know. My dad feels we need to read the New Testament because it was written by a Jewish kid from a small town that did well in life. The kid's name is Jesus, a nice Jewish name."

"You seem to have a scripture for everything."

"Well, not everything, but most of the important things. I know that scripture well because my dad has it plastered everywhere in the shop. And the ACLU has not taken him to court yet! The workers also like it."

"Hey, Christopher . . ." I have to use his full name since he does not like to be called Christ, or even Chris, because his sister's name is Chris! ". . . if you want a job at my father's company, just apply and I will put a good, no, a very good, word in for you."

"No, I want to make it on my own. My pride is at stake." Christopher responded in his usual honest self.

"Well, swallow your pride and let go of it so you can go to work!"

"No. I cannot do that!"

"Why not?"

"I just can't." Christopher answered, still resisting visiting the shop for reasons that eluded me.

"Well, try!"

"Hey, I have to get to class now. See you later, Billy. It was great talking to you," Christopher yelled as he began heading to his next class.

"Sure thing," I yelled back, adding, "I work after school at my dad's plant. I would like you to tag along with me sometime."

"Let me think about it."

"Okay. Great." Thinking about it was a good start, I reasoned. While walking to class, I met Lenny, another student in my class.

"Billy! Have you seen Sandy? She's filled out and looks great! What a beauty, always was. Now what a looker she is!"

"I haven't noticed."

"Well, you must be blind." Lenny shot back. I just looked at him.

"I heard she is trying out to be a cheerleader. I'm going to the game just to see her!" Lenny added.

Just being honest, I intoned: "She is way out of my league, and anyway, I hear she is dating the football quarterback."

"Billy, he's the fullback, not the quarterback."

"Well, whatever. I don't have any interest in football."

"That's obvious," Lenny remarked, explaining to me that, "The quarterback is the leader of the team. The center is the player who snaps the ball to the quarterback. The fullback is a player who's responsible for blocking for the running back guy and also for pass-blocking to protect the quarterback. Lastly, the running back is the player who runs with the football. Got it?"

"I think so. I'm not into football at all. What's the point?"

"The point is to win the game and earn the admiration of all the hot girls, that's what's the point."

"I'm glad some people like it. I don't," I explained, attempting to be as honest as possible.

"Well, you won't get a hot babe with that attitude."

"Maybe not. If a hot babe likes me only for my football skills and knowledge, I'm better off without her."

Lenny shot back, "Not me!"

"Well, I have to go to class now." I added, "See you later and good luck with the hot babes."

"Thanks. I'll need it!"

CHAPTER 4
Tenth-Grade Life in High School

L ike the stereotypical nerd, I was never involved in sports beyond that required for school. I did not even attend sporting events or follow a sports team, as did most persons my age. Part of the problem was I worked almost every afternoon for my dad. Another part was, I was not in the least athletically talented and, with good reason, I was almost always the last one picked for the required school athletic events. Sports was one activity where I was sure to fail in front of all my peers, and fail I almost always did—obviously a most embarrassing event.

In sixth grade, the boys in our class were divided up into two baseball teams for a special event. As usual, when we divided up into teams I was picked dead last. I went up to bat six times and struck out all six times and, as a result, our team lost. I knew our team lost because I never hit the ball even once. I felt horrible because I knew our team lost because of me. Being left-handed and batting right-handed didn't help. Not knowing any better, I imitated everyone else and batted the way they did.

Sports was a sore spot with me ever since, especially in high school. I now know one reason for my poor performance was my light-blue eyes. I have always been bothered by bright light and when playing outdoor sports I did not see too well. Where I got these eyes from I do not know. Everyone in my family has dark brown eyes. My doctor said it was a mutation like those in albinos, only a different gene.

My friends, after noting I never caught a ball when playing outfield, once asked, "Are you blind? How could you miss that ball? It fell right in front of you!"

Even my best friend Christopher chimed in, yelling to me, "Thanks a lot. We lost because of you! There was no way you could miss that one! It was like the ball was thrown right at you. And you missed it. You must be blind!"

Actually, I was blinded by bright lights and that included, especially, the sun. I am also partially color blind. For this reason, I always preferred indoor activities. This forced me to spend time inside reading books while my friends were outside playing various sports.

Only once in my life did I have a positive experience in sports. In high school, when preparing to run a mile for track in gym class, we were told to go easy at first so as to have enough energy to finish. I knew that I was a good runner, though, so for our gym class exercise I took off as fast as I could and ignored the coach's advice.

As I ran the third time around the quarter-mile-long track, I looked around and noticed no one was around me. Wondering where everyone was, I looked behind me and saw the entire class trailing me! I kept up my pace and, even though I was not in training, I finished well ahead of everyone else in the class.

When I completed the run I slowed down, as we were told to do, and a dozen or more of my fellow classmates yelled, "Way to go, Billy! WOW! Great job!" This was the first time—ever—that I earned praise for my athletic ability. The coach sat down with me and said, "We really need guys like you to go out for track. You are good, very good!"

"I would like to, but I have to work almost every day after school for my dad in the family business."

"Let me talk to your father. I will try to convince him how important sports are. They build bodies, teamwork and lead to important social experiences. You are that good. You may even earn a few awards, and your name will be in the local record books forever!"

"Really? Be in the record books? Then I will do it!"

He talked to my dad and I was on the team! I was active for the last two years of high school and won several awards. I even ended up with a minor college scholarship.

It was also the last time I was involved in a sport. I was never again able to excel at any sport, anywhere.

I fully understand from my one successful track experience why sports appeal to so many people. I later learned that people with my background are often good at track. They tend to have long, strong legs and thin upper frames (my father had the same build that I do), which is ideal for excelling in track.

As my mother advised me to, I took mostly shop classes in high school, plus I had four years of math: algebra, plane geometry, trigonometry, and calculus. I ended up being called a nerd for my math skills (my dad helped me a lot), a jock for my track records, a shop rat for my heavy load of industrial arts classes, and a snob because I was a "spoiled rich kid." They just could not figure me out! The most common label I was given, though, was a nerd. And I was that.

CHAPTER 5

My New Corvette

During the summer just before I started eleventh grade, I finally had earned enough money to make a down payment on my Corvette. It was a two-year-old model, a red convertible in new condition, costing over twelve-thousand dollars. I put five-thousand dollars down and had payments of hundred-fifty dollars a month.

After I bought my dream car, dad said, "Now I do not need to pick you up from school to drive you to work! But I do expect you to be at work on time! Got it?"

Dad then added, "The car is in my name, so I can take it away from you anytime. Just a warning. Behave and you will be fine."

"Dad, you know I always behave!"

"Yes, you do. That's why you drive an almost-new Corvette!"

"Thanks dad. Your trust means a lot to me. I know several of your friends strongly advised against letting me buy a Corvette, suggesting a ten-year-old Ford would do."

"I was your age once. I had to court your mom in my old car. Now you have a chick magnet!" my dad added.

"Dad! I am surprised to hear you say that!" I knew it was true. I heard rumors that the new girl at school, Bela, said if I got a Corvette, she would like to take a spin with me, and I planned on taking her up on it!

"Boy, I can't wait," I told dad.

"Well, you will have to," he answered, stressing I needed to have patience.

I had patience all right. I saved and saved until I had the down payment of five-thousand dollars. I had that to look forward to if my parents would sign for me. They did and I bought the car. I drove it to school and work every day.

A few months later, when at home, mom reminded me of our little talk we had last year that was about my obligation to my family and how to prepare to run the family business.

"How many kids at your school drive a Corvette?"

"None that I know of," I answered honestly.

"Has your car increased or decreased your popularity?" mom asked.

"Oh, it has rocketed upward since I bought my car. Even Bela, now the most popular girl in school, promised to take a spin with me. How about that?!" I added with a grin plastered all over my face.

"But what you want me to do, well, it's like bribery to get me to do what dad wants. I get the car, and, in return, I have to give my life to the plant," I told mom.

"Let's call it an enticement. Or, better yet, an encouragement," mom responded, hoping to make the deal sound less ominous.

Eleventh Grade Begins

"How was your summer, Christopher?" I asked, actually happy to be back.

"Fine, except I never did get my work permit, so I won't be working until next summer."

"Well, then you can take a trip with me to my dad's work and he can arrange to get the permit. He got my work permit last year. Had the company lawyer take care of those details."

"I guess that will work. Do I have a choice?"

"You do. Just don't bother working until you get the permit next year or so!"

Finally, I got my best friend, Christopher, to shadow me at the factory on one of my full workdays.

"Well, what do you do here?" Christopher asked when we met at the shop.

"I do a different job almost every day," I responded with pride in my work. "The goal is so I can eventually take over the operations of the plant. That requires me to understand the entire operation from the custodian's job duties to the president's.

"Wow!" Christopher replied, obviously impressed.

Today, I work with the quality control supervisor. He has me read the blueprints and then measure the parts produced to ensure they are within the required tolerances. I check every one-hundredth part and look for drifting values as I go through the parts. I've already learned how to use vernier calipers, and now I have to practice what I learned. The normal operator gets a much needed break when I do his job!"

"And what is the point?"

"To produce a good product and make my contribution to society."

"That's silly. Do you really enjoy working with vernier calipers or whatever they call them?"

"Yes, I do. I like mechanical things. I have been working with my dad since fourth grade."

After the end of the day, Christopher said, "I guess I would rather work for your dad's company than do nothing."

"Now you can save up for your Corvette?"

"Yeah, right. It will be a long time before I have enough money for a Corvette. I'll probably have to help my mom out. You know, she is divorced and things are very difficult now."

"I didn't know that. I feel sorry for you," I mentioned, sadly.

CHAPTER 6

Eleventh Grade and Bela

I was very busy during my last two years of high school. I was also still very shy, and rarely dated, even in eleventh grade. Most of the female students I've known since elementary school, so we saw each other more as brothers and sisters than potential boyfriends or girlfriends. My school was also small, less than thirty students in each grade. From a distance, I envied what we called "the lookers," the really attractive girls like Sandy, most of whom had boyfriends that were football or basketball stars. I was a track star and when we were out running there was no large stadium with hundreds of spectators there. It was not a rough and tumble sport like football. We just ran. Besides that, I did not really care to date anyone. My life was too full as it is.

Then Bela came along when I was in eleventh grade. She was stunning, my age, and had moved into a large fancy house near me. She always dressed to perfection. Perfect hair. Perfect makeup. Not too much, just enough to look great and natural. When she came, Sandy was left behind in the thoughts of many of the boys including me.

"I understand Bela is dating Sandy's old boyfriend," Christopher chimed in with the news.

I responded by adding, "That's what I heard. Sandy is very upset at being dumped."

Christopher agreed, adding, "You can't blame her, but no one knows much about Bela. I heard she is from California. Her father was, or is, a bigshot Hollywood producer, at least that's what Bela says."

"Well, one look at her and you don't need to learn anything else about her!" I opined.

"Even you the shy guy really noticed her. That is a first for you! This is the first time I have seen you noticing a girl!"

"I noticed Sandy, in case you haven't been paying much attention!"

"Oh, yes," Christopher surmised. "You did just before we left tenth grade last year."

"Have you dated Sandy yet?" I asked to carry on a conversation that really didn't interest me much.

"No I have not," Christopher confessed, adding "Well, have you dated Bela?"

"No. I asked her to visit me at my father's company, but she turned me down."

"Visiting your dad's company is not a very romantic date, is it?"

"I suppose not, but then I don't have much experience in dating, and I don't have a sister to give me some guidance. I'm an only child."

Then a miracle happened. Bela asked me if she could have a ride in my red Corvette! She was serious this time.

That evening I picked her up at her home and, while there, I met her mom. Bela told me she was separated or divorced from her father, so she and her mom lived there alone. It was a large, beautiful home for only two people. Her two-story Bavarian-style ranch house had some of the most elaborate furnishings I have ever seen.

When I met her mom I said, "I am very pleased to meet you! I am very charmed by your daughter. She is a very popular girl in school."

"Why thank you, Billy! She has spoken well of you. She says you are a very hard worker. I really admire that trait in a man. My ex-husband was also a very hard worker and has provided very well for me, even after we separated."

"Thank you, madam. My dad is my inspiration. He's training me to take over the family business. Actually, he has been grooming me since I was in fourth grade, so I am learning a lot about our company."

"What kind of business is he in?"

"His plant manufactures a lot of machines and other products for sale, mostly to other industrial companies. One example is they make a punch like a hole punch except it punches finger tabs in books like you see in dictionaries and Bibles. I have one of the punches in my car. Let me get it to show you."

I then ran out to my Vette to show her one. I thought to myself, I was very impressed with her mom. She seemed like a really nice lady.

When I returned, I brought the book tab punch to show her how it works. "This is very useful to mark catalogs or sales manuals. Tabs that stick out don't last long and rip off after use. This punch system does not have that problem." I felt very proud of my sales ability!

"And what else does your company make?"

"We make a lot of custom-fit pneumatic power tools for all phases of manufacturing. An example is a pneumatic bolt driver that can screw all the bolts in the engine head simultaneously. You just place each socket on the bolt head using the flexible drive and lower the drive down, turn it on, and, in the time it takes to drive one bolt in, you can drive six or eight bolts."

"And what does this unit cost?"

"They are all custom-made, so one unit, including the motor drive assembly, may cost several hundred dollars to as much as two-thousand dollars. They are expensive, but each drive has to produce the correct torque level."

"Torque? What in the world is that?" asked Bela's mom.

"Torque is the amount of force needed to achieve the correct tightness, not too tight or you will break the nut or bolt head off, and not too weak or the bolt will loosen as the engine runs. A lot of math is involved in designing these tools. If the system is not right, someone could get hurt and sue us, so it has to be right, actually close to perfect."

I continued, "We also make machines that drill, bore and tap, plus do other machining operations on parts mounted on a turret that turns and stops for the operation to be performed at each station. The operator places a part in the entry port, secures it, and turns the machine on. After it completes the circuit, up to forty machine operations are done automatically. If this process was done by hand, it would take as long as an hour or more with some down time. Also, the machines we make achieve tolerances well beyond that normally achievable by hand."

"And what do these machines cost?"

"Anywhere from several hundred to several million dollars."

"That's a lot of money. So what is the company's annual sales?"

"For all divisions, we are now at over three million dollars and growing." I had to wonder what the point was about all these questions, but I loved to talk about my company. I felt really good about my work. I was in my element and believe the work done by my dad's company was worthwhile.

Then Bela interrupted us and said to her mom, "Billy is my date and we need to get going. His Vette is outside waiting for me." I thought she was somewhat rude, but we did need to get going.

So off we went to visit the company. I was very comfortable with Bela when in my element, not so comfortable in other elements, like sports. I had a great time showing her around the factory and she seemed very impressed. I thought to myself, I really like this girl. This was the first girl I felt this way about and very much looked forward to doing things with her again.

CHAPTER 7

Bela and the Wrestling Match

A t the factory we had a great time. I loved showing off my work and knowledge. Bela seemed very interested in the money end of the business, as was her mother, and asked a lot of questions. How much is the company worth? How much did I make? What was my future with the company? I appreciated her interest in me and thought if I could have a girl like Bela, it would be my dream come true; me, a guy who rarely dated anyone! On the other hand, she seemed less interested in me than in my future, at least that was my presumption.

Maybe I was being a bit too sensitive.

Later, when I mentioned this to my mom, she said, "You remember that multi-national survey I told you about?"

"Vaguely, to be honest."

"The most important trait that both men and women in the dozen countries that were part of the survey looked for in a mate was simple kindness. The second most important trait they looked for in a mate was a world apart for males and females."

"Okay. What was the second most important trait they looked for?"

"For males, it was appearance, beauty, and attractiveness."

"And what was it for females?"

"Security, a man's ability to support her. Is the man a good worker? A good provider? Does he have potential as a husband and provider?"

"Mom, I'm in high school and not thinking of marrying anyone for some time."

"I was young when I married your father."

"Mother, that was a long time ago in England. Kids do not want to marry in America until they have their career established."

"I know, but they should at least be thinking of their future."

"I am, but I am not thinking that far into the future! I am now just thinking of graduating from high school."

I dated Bela on and off for the next year. I constantly got mixed feelings about her. If where we were going required driving, she wanted to go with me; but she talked a lot about Butch, the guy in the gym who spent much of his time weight-lifting, who was the quarterback on the football team and also was a wrestler.

In our small school there were only a few guys on the wrestling team. One was injured at the last football game and the other was ill with mononucleosis. That left Butch. He had consistently defeated everyone else, so we held the division meet anyway to pick the winner of our local division. Bela wanted to be there, but she did not want to ride with Butch in his twelve-year-old Ford.

"I'm afraid his car will not make it," Bela claimed. "Last time I rode with him we ended up walking part way to the event we were going to."

"What if both of you ride with me?" I asked, feeling that was a logical solution to the problem.

"In your two seater Vette? Where am I supposed to sit? In the trunk?" Bela asked with a puzzled look on her face.

"I can borrow my father's car. He has a Mercedes with plenty of room."

"No, I want to go to the match with you in your car." So, she rode with me, and the guy she went to watch wrestle, Butch, went by himself to the match.

Butch, not his real name, but that was the name we called him, was probably one of the best wrestlers in the state. His name was actually Rodney. After a few wrestling matches when he triumphed over all of his opponents at the school, and moved on to wrestling at other schools, he was called Butch ever since. The name fit him much better than Rodney.

When we arrived, Bela, proudly perched up in my Corvette convertible, was the hit of her friends and students from the other school. Also a few of the students from the other school were waiting to watch this widely publicized match for the regional championship. Butch was already inside getting ready to defend his title.

Even I was looking forward to the performance, although I knew next to nothing about wrestling, or actually any sport.

On the way there, I noticed Bela had a brown bag that had a bottle in it. The bottle label said root beer, which I found out later was alcohol. I did not drink any alcoholic beverages, so I thought this strange. She occasionally went out to the car for something, which I now know was for a drink. A lot of the kids at my school drank alcohol, so I thought little about it. I was having a great time with her. Bela was really great fun to be around. She made me feel like a star.

CHAPTER 8
The Fight

The start of the match was very slow, almost like a movie playing at slow speed. It seemed very obvious that the two combatants were close to evenly matched.

Butch seemed to have a slight edge, but not enough to pin his opponent. The tension rose, and our small school was looking to achieve some glory in this one area. Many of our teachers were there, as were many of our students.

Bela was getting more animated as each second the match progressed. Soon, at an intense time in the match, she burst forth a paroxysm of raw emotion I had never seen in her.

"Butch, COME ON! Let's GO! Pin him! Force his arm DOWN! Move now!!" Bela was yelling at the top of her lungs. She was really into this! I just sat there, hoping we would win one for our school, but I was not going berserk while watching the action.

"Butch, MOVE! Pin him now! COME ON!!" Looking at me she said, "What's your problem?"

"This is the first time I've been to a wrestling match, or any sports event." I said. She looked at me like I was out of my mind, then resumed her yelling. "GO For IT NOW, you almost had him pinned! Watch his left arm. GRAB IT!!" Bela yelled, going berserk again.

I never saw anything like it. I wanted us to win, but the raw emotion she and others invested was enormous.

"Look out for his right arm. WATCH IT, he's going to grab YOUR LEG!"

In the end, Butch won the title! I was very happy, but after the event was over the fights outside began.

"Butch, you cheated! This match was not fair and square," came the taunts. The police were there, expecting this after the highly contested event, and moved in quickly but not without some injuries.

"Cheaters! Butch was on speed. I saw him take something in the locker room!" One student yelled to the crowd.

Bela told me Butch had some allergies and he took medicine for it. "It wasn't speed," she added.

After several students were arrested, including one from our school, we were able to get out of the parking lot and drive home. On the way home, Bela was very quiet so I tried to cheer her up.

"You know, I was admiring my car and noticed it looks 100% better with you in it. You should think about doing some modeling. My dad pays good money for the pictures used in our product catalogues, and we could request the photo agency we use to hire you. It's a start."

"Do you really think so?" Bela asked with her usual quizzical look. "I don't think so, I know so!" I added firmly.

"I will talk to my father and arrange some introduction shoots."

"Would you really do this for me?"

"Yes, of course, I will. Look, Bela, I really enjoy being with you, and will do what I can to help you spend more time with me."

"That's very nice for you to say," Bela added while flashing a warm inviting smile. Her pleasant smile made me feel fantastic!

Then she added, "Thank you for the compliment!"

"You're very welcome!" I mouthed with a very snuggly smile.

I have to admit I was really getting to like this gal. I felt wonderful when I was with her. I remembered what my dad had told me over and over about how he fell madly in love with my mom. When he met her, he was hooked, and I mean "hook, line, and sinker"—hooked! He was young and so was she. I am seventeen now.

When I dropped Bela off at her home, I was anxiously expecting a kiss or at least a friendly hug, as I saw in the movies. I walked her up to the door and stood there for a few seconds, but she already had her key in the door and it was open before I knew it. She thanked me and was inside, closing the door in my face. I stood there for a few seconds somewhat mystified. I had no experience in the boy-girl department, so did not know what to think. I thought I needed to be optimistic, so just told myself that I was blessed to spend the time with her that I did. I forced myself to be thankful for the day and evening, and looked forward to tomorrow. After all, most guys would give their right arm to spend an evening with her. As my dad would say, "Count your blessings, son!"

I smiled and got in my car and drove home. Then I told dad what a great time I had!

He said, "Son, I am proud of you!! Bela is a great young lady and I am happy that you two get along so well."

"Thanks, dad. I knew you would be supportive. Say, can I ask a favor?"

"Sure son, anything."

"I suggested to Bela that she could earn some extra money if she did some modeling. I proposed that she do some work for the agency we use for publicity."

"I think that is a great idea. I will call them and suggest some test shots. We are a major client of their's and I hope they will endeavor to keep us as a client. If they have any business acumen they will follow our suggestion!" The next day, dad called them, and they explained, "Sure, we will be glad to give her a shot. We can always use some young, attractive models. Send her over for some test shots."

As soon as I got the okay, I stopped by her house and gave her directions to the studio for the test shots. She was so excited. "Oh, that's wonderful! Thank you!" she exclaimed, as she gave me a big hug and a kiss.

My first kiss! I was in heaven. Never have I felt like this! I was hopeful that our relationship could continue to develop. I felt I finally had a girlfriend! My first one, my only one.

Bela kept the appointment, dressed modestly as they suggested, and completed the poses and other photo shoots they wanted. The photographer explained that she would pose for a wide variety of pictures: women's clothes, women's accessories like purses, bags, shoes, and jewelry, and even machinery, cars, and the other work they did for their clients.

Bela's pictures came out perfectly. Within days, she got some modeling work. Soon her picture was in ads published in the newspaper, in catalogues, and also in local stores showing off their products.

"Thank you, Billy! You have done this for me and I really appreciate your help and support!"

"You're welcome," I told her. "I was glad to help. Very glad." She rarely seemed to appreciate what I did for her, so I felt awesome from this compliment. It is nice to get a compliment occasionally. Very nice, especially from Bela.

CHAPTER 9
Senior Homecoming Queen

We all knew Bela would be the homecoming queen this year, and I knew I had no chance of being homecoming king. Butch got it, which surprised no one, not even me. I dreamed I would, but knew that it was a long shot, a very long shot.

At the ceremony, when introduced to the school, Bela gave Butch a big wet kiss. I was livid, and disappointed. Very disappointed. That seemed to be my life with her. In Heaven one minute and pain in the next.

I took Bela to the dance and, again, she seemed to pay more attention to the other guys than to me.

Christopher responded to my complaints, "What do you expect? She's the most popular girl in the school, by far. Gorgeous, friendly to a fault, great sense of humor, and a face that launched a thousand ships, or was it a hundred ships?"

"I'm sure it was a thousand!" I responded, a little downcast.

Christopher then added, "You are the lucky guy, the envy of every guy in the school. Don't complain!!! I'm lucky if she just says hi to me," Christopher remarked.

"You're right. I'm blessed, and should stop fretting." Christopher was a good friend, and I knew I was blessed by him. I just needed to appreciate what I had.

Later that evening, I mentioned to Bela her long kiss with Butch in front of the entire school.

"We never kiss like that," I explained and added, trying to put some humor into my complaint, "Maybe you could give me some lessons!"

"You are not funny," is all she said. I just tried to smile, but inside I was hurt . . . again.

I relayed my experience to Christopher. As usual, he tried to help me feel good about my attempt to be humorous.

"She probably was embarrassed about your comment. Some girls are like that, so don't take it seriously," Christopher answered in his usual supportive role in our friendship.

"I appreciate your very positive outlook on life. Where do you get this outlook on life?"

"Do you really want to know?'

"Yes," I answered, really curious and not knowing what answer I would get.

"My small church support group."

"Really?"

"Yes, really."

"Where is your meeting?

"We meet in a private home once a month. We rotate, meeting in Curtis' home one month, then in my home the next month. Actually, we'll be meeting in my home next month. You are welcome to come. You know where I live don't you?"

"Obviously. I've been there enough times. Tell me what time you start and I'll be there."

"Seven o'clock sharp on the first Friday of the month," Christopher answered.

"I will be there, but I am Jewish, or my family was. Will that be a problem?"

"Heavens, no. That will be a challenge! We have great fellowship, usually ten to twelve attend. We do a Bible study, in both the Old and New Testaments, or show a film or have discussions, have a snack, and fellowship for an hour or two."

I started regularly attending, and this fellowship changed my life. These people were a godsend. I had to field a lot of questions about Jews, most of which I couldn't answer. The closest synagogue was almost two hours away so we rarely could attend. We were mostly lapsed Jews anyway, as are many in the Western world. I am from a family of rabbis but our family then became secular Jews. That was our story, as is true of most Western Jews. I also began attending their church, sporadically at first, then more regularly in time.

CHAPTER 10

My Father Dies

C lose to the last month of my senior year, my father died. It was a heart attack. The previous heart damage from the injury in the hunting accident finally did him in. We were devastated, but not all that surprised. We had been expecting this outcome of the hunting accident for some time.

He had an enormous funeral. Over five-hundred people came, mostly the company's workers and their families. Rebekah Martin was also there. She thanked me for the umpteenth time for the financial help my father gave her to get through nursing school. She came from a poor family, and I knew she would not have had a nursing career without his help. She knew it as well and was very thankful. Her daughter, Angela, was also there. Angela was a stunner, the life of the party without even trying.

Bela didn't want to come, though. "I hate funerals," she said. "They make me sad, depressed and bother me."

"What about the support for the family? Is that not important?" I asked. Disappointed, I went alone. Numerous people asked about Bela. I said, "She's not feeling well." Several felt that was a very lame excuse. So did I. Bela seemed to have two sides to her: the loving sweet side and the mean, nasty, selfish side. Then I guess we all do at times, so I moved on to thinking about good thoughts about my father.

Then one guest, Cindy, who worked in the accounting department, popped up and offered her thoughts. "I was diagnosed with cancer several months ago, and am now undergoing chemotherapy. Still, I came in respect of a wonderful boss and man. Your dad gave Bela a lot of work, helped her earn good money for some fun work, if you can call it work. You'd think she would have the respect to attend his funeral."

Due to my dad's passing, I was installed as the president of the company. I was almost eighteen years old, but had trained for this role since I was in elementary school. My appointment was not unexpected and I had dozens of people stop by to congratulate me.

"Billy, you're the best man for the job, without a doubt!" Dick Courtney, our production manager, said to me flashing his warm smile. "Of course I am! I was trained by the best there is. You! So if you don't like a decision I make I can blame it on you! Seriously, if you don't like a decision I make, I will always be open to discussion, just as I have been in the past when I had no authority!"

"I know you are easy to work with, and so I feel very comfortable working with you, even though you are younger than my youngest son!"

"Only by a few months!" I added. "And you have always been like a second father to me."

"I really appreciate that compliment!" Dick almost whispered to me with a smile plastered all over his face. He then added, "I wish my own son was a little more respectful."

"He will. Just give him more time. I had to grow up fast because we all knew this day was coming. Now here it is."

With that he gave me a hug and went back to work.

CHAPTER 11

What to Do About School

I had more than a month left of high school, so met with the superintendent, Dr. Lamphere, to make arrangements to graduate. I decided to use my business finesse, and so invited him to lunch in the boardroom of the plant. After lunch, I showed him around the plant and gave him a chance to meet some of the workers.

He was very impressed with everything. Then I raised the problem of my graduation. "I have to run the corporation, especially when I now must deal with the transition from my father to me," I added, waiting for his response.

"I understand. This problem is very unusual, in fact I've never run into it in my 32 years as a superintendent," he stated in his deep, authoritative voice.

"Actually, I have been thinking about this ever since I became aware of the problem that your transition created. We still want you to be listed as a graduate of Germantown High, not as a Germantown student who never graduated, or worse, one who dropped out of school to run a large corporation. Do you see the problem?!"

"I certainly do!" I replied reflecting understanding in my voice.

"As a graduate of the school, Dr. Lamphere noted, you will add to our prestige and that of the district. We were thinking of a work study assignment which we sometimes use for students who have to miss classes due to illness. This assignment would involve a presentation in the school gymnasium for all of the high school students. You'd be graded on your performance and given credit. You could also give the seniors and juniors a tour of your factory. You've certainly demonstrated to me today your ability to do an excellent job as a tour guide."

"Thank you! I have been training for this role since fourth grade," I explained.

I agreed with the requirement and was glad he didn't say, "Forget the last month or so of schoolwork. We'll just give you your diploma with honors and move on." I had a 4.0 average up to that time.

Within two weeks I completed the tours, and, in another week, I completed the school assembly assignment. I felt, instead of being the oddball in school, I could now be an inspiration to other students! Life was good now, very good for me.

CHAPTER 12

Soon Commencement Came

B ela and I went to the senior prom, and afterwards I felt wonderful. I never was so happy in all my life but felt Bela seemed distant. She often did.

I was tired and tried to be as much fun as possible, complimenting her at every turn.

"It's just her time of the month," I was told. "Accept it. It happens once a month. Women sometimes are hard to get along with at this time. You're a better person if you are understanding." I thought I was, or tried to be understanding, and moved on.

Next was commencement, the party afterward, and visits from well-wishers.

After graduation, after thinking long and hard about my future, I proposed to her.

She smiled and responded by saying "You are a very sweet guy, Billy, one of the nicest guys I have ever met in my life, but I have bigger plans. My father is living in Hollywood and he's got me an audition with a very famous producer. I'm going to Hollywood and I'm going to be a big star. My skill will take me to the top. I will be acting with famous and glamorous stars. I have all the connections now. This is my life's calling. It is what I was destined to do."

And with that, she left. I was devastated. I would have to get back to my humdrum life. My mother said, "You have a lot to offer and will find some nice girl and settle down. Might not be the ideal woman of your dreams, but a very nice girl."

I did not want to find a nice girl. I already had a nice girl, a wonderful girl. And I did not want to lose her, not now, and not in a million years.

My mother added, I suppose to cheer me up, that "a girl who is attracted to a guy for his nice car is not the kind of girl you want to attract." Her opinion didn't help me much.

Occasionally I'd visit Bela's mother as a way of connecting with Bela. "So, what's the word about Bela," I asked once.

"She has had several appointments with directors for movie parts."

"That's great!" I told her, attempting to make the best of the situation.

"In the meantime, she's doing a lot of modeling to get by, waiting for her big break."

I was proud of her, but missed her terribly.

Later, when I told the latest news about Bela to Christopher, he said what he'd said several times before: "You dated her for a year. I never had one lousy date with her, so don't complain. You're eighteen now, the head of a multi-billion-dollar corporation, and you're in the dumps about some girl! Get real, and get your priorities straightened out."

I thought I was, to some degree, a figurehead, not really the head of a multi-billion-dollar corporation. The corporation is run by a Board of Directors and a large staff of department heads and workers. And it wasn't quite a multi-billion dollar corporation.

"She is not just some girl, but the most beautiful, wonderful, smartest, nicest girl in the world."

"That's a judgment, your judgment," Christopher replied.

"Not just my judgment; the judgment of the entire school. She was homecoming queen."

"Yes, you've said that a zillion times. You really miss her, don't you?"

"Yes, I do."

"Then why don't you fly out to see her?" You could make it a business trip, and maybe meet with a few customers while you're out there."

"Great idea! I will do that this week."

CHAPTER 13
Flying to California

I arranged a trip to Thousand Oaks, California to meet with a director of a corporation that we had done a lot of work for. In a week it was all set up. I landed at the Los Angeles Airport and an employee of the company picked me up.

We had a very productive meeting. When I was there, the local business news station decided to do a story on one of the youngest business executives in the country, me. The story also made the front page of the L.A. Times.

The next day, I received a call from Bela's father! He'd read the story in the L.A. Times and recognized the company I was head of and looked it up. Sure enough, he discovered I had dated his daughter, and invited me to meet him, which I did. He explained he felt some misunderstanding existed between him and his ex-wife. I told him what I knew and he explained his side, just in case I became his son-in-law.

"Well, there's a lot you don't know. Bela's mother left me. I did not want the divorce. She did. Our story also received a lot of publicity. I had to pay her almost two million dollars, which she blew on who knows what. She went back to court and I had to buy her a house to take care of my daughter."

"How about the important producers you fixed Bela up with?" I asked.

"I did not set my daughter up with any big producers. I am a small-time writer and most of my savings are gone, thanks to my ex-wife. I get by from rewriting movie scripts for the big screen, so cannot complain. Most people in Hollywood do not have a clue about me and what I do. I am one of the many people who work silently behind the scenes."

"You mean she was lying?"

"That's exactly what I mean. I could not set her up with any important producers even if I wanted to. I'm an independent contractor and do not know any producers, at least not firsthand. I told you I work for the scriptwriters, preparing scripts for the movie. I do a lot of editing for the main editor that heads the film production department.

"Why would Bela lie about you?" I asked, very disappointed in her.

"I have no idea why," her father responded as he raised his shoulders to emphasize his point.

"Can I see her? Do you know where she lives?"

"No, but I can find out. I didn't even know she was here in Hollywood!"

"Well, now you know! I'll keep in touch with you," I said, as I left for more meetings with past and present clients.

I had to admit, I really liked that man. I felt good about him the first time I met him. I also had to wonder about Bela's mother.

I finally was able to meet up with Bela. The first thing I said to her was "I met your father. He seems like a very nice person."

"He seems like he is, that is if you don't know him, but he is not by a long shot. He dumped my mother, and for that I will never forgive him," she explained.

I soon realized her picture was very different than what I'd learned from him, but did not want to press the issue.

"How are you doing, is the question," I added trying to change the topic.

"To be honest, not well. I've talked to a number of producers and so far, nothing except a lot of hints, or, more often invitations to spend some time on the casting couch. Accepting their proposals made me realize that the promised offers of a part often don't seem to follow my performance, if you know what I mean." I would only later find out what she meant by the casting couch.

"Don't give up!" I said. "Keep working to pursue your dream," I added, always attempting to be upbeat.

"I know you'll make it. You have the talent, the beauty, and the brains to make it really big! I've seen you act in school plays, so, although I am very biased, I speak from my experience watching you act. You were great! No, incredible, and you have a very promising career ahead of you."

"I appreciate your confidence in me, Billy. You've always been encouraging, building me up, and kind to a fault."

"And I always will be," I added, smiling.

"When I interviewed with agencies, the response was always: 'There are thirty-thousand high schools in the United States and each has a homecoming queen. That means in four years we have one-hundred and twenty-thousand, and in ten years, three-hundred thousand homecoming queens. And it seems most every one of these girls thinks she can become a big movie star. We have, maybe, at most, ten new female stars a year, and many of them have some exceptional talent, like voice or another musical skill.'"

"I never saw it that way," I remarked.

"The fact is, you give in or quit, so I applied for more modeling jobs."

"How did it go?"

"Not so well, to be honest."

At that, Bela's roommate, another aspiring actress, piped in. "I was told they always have a need for new nude models. The career is short. Doesn't require any acting ability, and you get paid thirty to thirty-five dollars an hour. You may work for three hours at the most, so that's one-hundred and five dollars a day."

"How much do you make?" I asked.

"Usually not more than two-hundred dollars a day."

"And how much a year?"

"It depends on how long you last. The sales and show view numbers are recorded, and if you start to fall in views as I did, you have to look for something else to pay the bills. It's very competitive. A lot of the work is done by husbands operating the camera and their wife working as the model. These working couples also cut the price enormously. They may do well for a few months, but few last very long. Both still photos and movies are done now. Any stretch marks and appendix scars and that's usually the end of your career. Most girls are young, sixteen to twenty or so."

"Isn't that illegal?"

"Sure, but who's going to watch pornography all day and try to pick out the underage girls and go after them? You can't tell by looking at them how old they are. Some are sixteen and look like they're twenty-two. Some are twenty-two and look like they're sixteen. It's not worth the time to go after them. This is a five million-dollar business. Also, a lot of pictures are shot in Europe and other countries. We can't do anything to them in America."

"What about the lawsuits I've read about?"

"In some of those cases, some young woman gains too much weight, gets let go, and decides to sue."

My thought was, "This is a sleazy business, but that's what we all knew. That's Hollywood."

I turned to Bela and said, "You can always come home. My marriage proposal is still good if you want to take that route."

A month later she called me. "I've had it here," she said. "I've already had far too many bad experiences. This is an immoral, sleazy place."

"I feel bad for you, Bela. You will do well if you can just get your big break," I added, always the optimist. I was told more than once that my overconfidence would, in the end, get me into trouble. I hope not.

"I really appreciate your confidence in me. I really do," Bela answered.

"Thank you. I've always loved you, and I always will," I added. "Billy, I want to accept your marriage proposal now."

"Are you serious?"

"Yes. I'm very serious."

"Well, come home and we'll start planning for the wedding!"

"I have been out here for almost a year and I'm broke. I've used up all my savings and I was never paid for several jobs I did. And I'm tired of asking for the money I earned."

"Don't worry. I'll wire you as much money as you need. Will two-thousand do?"

"That will be great. You really are a wonderful guy."

I wired her the money and she was on the next plane home.

CHAPTER 14
The Wedding

Although Jewish in ethnicity, I'd attended the Baptist Church due to Christopher's influence in high school. I became a Messianic Jew, an ethnic Jew that became a Christian. My faith must have rubbed off on him as Christopher, a former skeptic, became a committed Christian believer. He then influenced me to attend church. I guess actually we influenced each other to become more involved in Christianity! I'd learned a lot about how the over three-hundred prophecies in our own Jewish Old Testament could point to one Person, that of the Jew, Jesus.

We were married in my church. As expected, the church was packed. My vows were:

> "I, Billy, do take you, Bela, to be my lawfully wedded wife after God's ordinance, in the holy estate of matrimony. To have and to hold from this day forward, for better or for worse, for richer or for poorer, in life. As God is my witness, I give you this promise."

Bela's vows: were as follows

"I, Bela, do take you, Billy, to be my lawfully wedded husband after God's ordinance, in the holy estate of matrimony. To have and to hold from this day forward, for better or for worse, for richer or for poorer, in sickness and in health. I will love you and cherish you all the days of my life. As God is my witness, I give you this promise."

Bela was as sweet as I had ever seen her. She'd matured a lot in the past year and it was obvious that she was ready to assume the responsibility of marriage. She was my first girl . . . and my only girl. And now, she was my wife. I was overjoyed, filled with love which would never change in spite of some difficulties we would experience which lie ahead.

We decided to use the company auditorium for the reception because it was the only local room that was able to hold all of the guests we expected. The entire plant staff was invited. That way, too, we would not have the problem of certain people not wanting to go to a wedding reception in a building of a different denomination. Besides that, most of those attending would be people I'd worked with.

After the reception, we moved into a townhouse until our new house in the best part of town was finished. We hired an architect and Bela took an active part in all phases of the design and construction. It was a two-story, Bavarian-style, four-thousand-square-foot home. It had four bedrooms, three baths, a large library, a roomy kitchen, and three walk-in closets. Bela called it a mansion and it was.

I felt wonderful. I had a great job, a great wife, and a beautiful home located in Mansion Row next to doctors, lawyers, and the best of society. I had never dreamed of the life I-sorry, we—my wife and I, now enjoyed.

Soon we had two children, both boys. Bela and the boys were my life, my wonderful life. I spent a lot of time with them, as much as I could, even taking the boys to work with me attempting to explain what I did for a living.

Bela did what was necessary to take care of the boys, but seemed to view it as a burden that was in the way of what she wanted to do, so we hired a housekeeper who ended up as their main caretaker. I ended up being their main parent.

Once, my older boy, who was almost five, asked: "Daddy, why do you make all these things, like this tab punch, and then sell them? Why don't people who want a tab punch just make one for themselves?"

"For one thing, they don't have all the needed tools to do so." My precious son in his sweet child voice then asked "Well, they could buy the tools and then make their own tab punch, couldn't they?"

"They could, but they may not know all of the details of how to make it."

"You could teach them like you are doing for me now!"

"Then how could I earn the money to buy the magic kits I buy for you?" I answered.

"They could pay you to show them how to make the tab punch."

"It's a lot less expensive to just make them here in the factory. We need to move on now, son, but you have some really good questions!"

When the boys were born, I wanted them to attend our church to help them accept the Christian faith as a moral foundation for their life.

When I told Bela about my intentions she sternly replied, "No way, I'm going to a church," Bela retorted. "They're all a bunch of hypocrites. In Hollywood they would piously attend on Sunday, then throw off all moral restraint for the rest of the week. Besides that, I learned about evolution in high school. Because we evolved, what's the point of God? I know they teach He nudged evolution at certain times, but we have all the links between modern man and our monkey ancestors. So, what did God do? It seems science has proven God is not necessary anymore."

I could not answer these concerns and did not even try. I did wonder why the pastor did not answer them, though, at least I do not remember them being covered in the few years I'd been going to church.

"Churches marry people and bury people. If you are not being married or buried, why waste your time going?" Bela stated as she began walking out of the room.

She continued, "Once I believed in God, but my science high school classes took care of that. Did you have Mr. Martin for any class?"

"No. I never had him."

"He was an excellent teacher and showed why God is a fairy tale for grown-ups. We had a lot of good discussions in his class. Some of the students attempted to give reasons for why they believed in God, but Mr. Martin very effectively shot them all down. He's a very smart man!"

CHAPTER 15
Problems in Marriage

Not long after this conversation, trouble reared its ugly head. I noticed money was missing from my wall safe, not just a few dollars, but hundreds of dollars. Bela had the combination so I knew she took it. "Honey, if you need money for expenses, please just ask, but I need to keep track of things. I am also concerned that maybe the help is again stealing money."

"It must be the help, darling. You know I am very careful about money. I had little when growing up so I appreciate what I have now."

Unknown to anyone else, I set up a security system. I had to let the last housekeeper go because of this problem. Letting her go really hurt the boys, but we felt we had no choice. The housekeeper insisted she did not take the money but I believed my wife, not her. I now think I might have made a mistake.

I also noted Bela had managed her own expense budget and was far overspending it, and I wanted to find out why. Was she buying very expensive jewelry? What was she using all this money for? I was at a complete loss as to what she was using thousands of dollars for, and what the money was being spent on.

The video system was connected to my office at the plant. About a week after I set it up, I saw my wife in the safe taking out several hundred dollars. I gave her the combination so she could get in there at will. The help did not have the combination, but sometimes Bela or I left it open.

After the fifth time watching her take out hundreds of dollars, I felt I had to do something. What was she spending all that money on?

When I confronted her, I mentioned I wanted to determine if the help was stealing money. Instead, I found out from the security cameras that she was, and I was probably wrong for blaming the last loss on the help.

Bela was very upset when I mentioned this concern to her. She protested, "My own husband is accusing me of this?! What kind of man are you?"

"No, I wasn't attempting to entrap you. I was trying to catch the help whom I suspected of doing it, and I needed proof. But, I looked at the checkbook and noticed you spent almost 6,000 dollars last month which was unaccounted for. Most of the checks were made out to CASH. What are you doing? What in the world are you spending all that money on?"

"I am just spending money for the few pleasures I have in life. Is that a problem for you? You said you loved me, and now you're treating me like I'm a crook. I am extremely upset at you!"

"I have a very good income, but at this rate we will be bankrupt in a few years!" I explained to her with a level of anger I rarely displayed to anyone. I rarely ever got angry and my anger surprised even me.

"You run the company, so just give yourself a big raise," Bela calmly opined.

"You know the Board sets my salary and I cannot justify a significant raise."

I then took over our finances, including paying of all our bills. I even took the checkbook away from her and kept most of the cash that was in the safe in the locked cabinet in my office. I had the only key so she could not abscond with money from my office location. I also did all of our banking at the office.

When I asked a coworker about my suspicions, she said, "You're naive. She's on illegal drugs. All of the signs you related to me fit the pattern perfectly."

I had noticed what I thought was drug paraphernalia in the house. Then Christopher, who was now a detective, came to my office. "I have to talk to you, Billy. She is spending all that money for illegal drugs. Wake up to this fact. Your wife is buying drugs big-time in the sleazy part of town."

I now knew we had a big problem. A BIG problem.

About this time Bela got a job working for a Mr. Stromberg in a materials supply house that my plant bought supplies from. Soon strangers began to frequent our house.

"You've cut off my income, so I'm earning a little extra money on the side," she explained sheepishly.

"How are you doing that?" I asked her.

"Don't be so naïve. What do you think I am doing? I learned a lot in Hollywood. One thing I learned is how to exploit men and I'm just taking advantage of this fact."

Although I tried repeatedly, it became obvious that I could not reason with her about what she was doing. I kept thinking she would come to her senses.

One guy, a big muscle-bound African American man, would frequent the house. When he came, he'd yell at me, calling me "Bones" and, smiling, once said to me: "You're a blind fool."

After this event, I trained the cameras toward the entrance to the house and on several rooms.

When watching the camera footage, I noticed another man often came in. I recognized him as Mr. Stromberg, the man she was working for. Bela was overtly fawning over him.

When I confronted my wife about these events, she retorted, "Don't I deserve a little pleasure? I don't get much pleasure from you."

"Of course you deserve pleasure. You have a husband who loves you and we have two boys who are the light of our life."

"You are totally ignorant. You always have been a very naïve man. It should be obvious that you are not the father of those two boys."

I was dumbfounded! I did not know what to say. I'd seen this coming for at least the last two or three years, but had denied it up to now. I now had no choice but to face what was happening.

Angry, I said something I should have never said: "I am at a loss at how to deal with your drug and other problems. I may have to file for divorce unless things drastically change."

"Go ahead. File for divorce. I've already consulted with an attorney. He will take the case for free. He would love to go after you. Remember the Turner case? You sued and he lost big time. He's angry about what happened and wants to get back at you. He will demand, for me, half the company and half of everything you own, plus half of everything you will ever own. Go ahead and file. The headlines sure to come will help my case: Philandering husband divorces innocent wife. Go ahead and file. Be my guest!" she screamed.

In the meantime, Bela's attorney filed a lawsuit against the man she was working for, a man with a fair amount of money, for unwanted sexual attention. I was flabbergasted. It was in all the papers as what many years later would be referred to as the "Me Too Movement."

"We Need to Stop These Male Predators from Taking Advantage of Women," the headline read, showing a picture of my wife and, I was shocked to see, Mr. Stromberg!

When I saw his picture in the paper, I recognized him as the man, that, it appeared to me, she was openly pursuing. I was angry and contacted him, explaining I would be glad to appear in court on *his* side. He stopped by my office and told me the whole story. I got the name of his attorney and invited him to watch the tapes. In the meantime, *his* wife filed for divorce due to the press and lawsuit filed by Bela.

I then confronted Bela about it.

"He's just another ignorant man hitting on an innocent woman who worked for him."

"You know this charge is a lie."

"Who cares? The whole Women's Movement will be behind me. Who will the jury believe? A wronged innocent woman, or some rich, lecherous man? Women are tired of being abused by men with overactive testosterone. I certainly am."

"This is wrong and you know it." I shot back, now livid at what she was doing to me and other men.

"'Wrong?' You're so pathetic. You should know I married you for your money, but you were too ignorant to realize it. I never loved you, Bones. Get a life."

The national press about the lawsuit resulted in Bela's father calling me. He said he was going to testify against his own daughter. He flew in from L.A. and I picked him up at the airport. He talked to Bela and she was very upset. She now realized the whole world was closing in on her.

About this time, I learned from Christopher that she was a heroin addict spending as much as four-thousand dollars a week for illegal drugs. At least that is what he surmised she was spending. He told me they were closing in on the drug dealers who were selling to her, and Bela may be part of the sting.

So many of us tried to help her, but she would not listen, retaliating with, "What I do is my business, so butt out."

She pushed ahead with the lawsuits, hoping to make a fortune. "You men will pay for what you've done to women," she said more than once. "We, or at least I, would soon pay very dearly."

I was at a point where I had to do something drastic now. So I bluntly told her what I was now facing, "Bela, the corporation just had a board meeting about my situation. They are considering terminating me. That means I am out of the company and my income will be cut off. I may get a small severance pay, but that's all."

"What does that have to do with me? It's not my fault you're incompetent and you can't do your job."

"It has nothing to do with incompetence."

"Well, then, what's the problem?"

"In a nutshell, the problem is you."

"Me? How so?"

"They know you are a drug addict and have been stealing money from me and many others, and also prostituting yourself. This behavior, as my wife, reflects very poorly on me and the company. You have been using our house for these activities. I have defended you ever since I have known you, Bela, but I cannot defend you any longer. It is also in a major way adversely affecting our children."

"They're MY children. I told you, you are not the father, as you should know, you ignorant man."

"They are my children no matter what you say, and I will not allow you to ruin their lives, EVER. I love them far too much, even if you don't."

"So, what does the Board want you to do?"

"They want me to get a legal separation, for you to move out of my house, and agree to go into a drug rehabilitation center."

"And if I refuse?"

"I will get a court order to force you out. I've had it with you."

"And I thought you loved me!"

"I did, and still do, even after all of this. I will pay for your apartment and give you a stipend. I will also pay for the drug treatment costs. I will do whatever I can to get my wife back."

"If you try that, I will fight it in court."

"And who will defend you? I will cut off all your money and you will have to rely on whatever means you have, mostly stealing and prostitution, I assume. I have no choice now. We will both lose everything if I do nothing. I have to do something, and now. I will not let the lives of our children, and both you and me, be ruined, and that is where we are at now."

"Is that how you treat me after all I've done for you?" Bela screamed at me.

"You know what has to be done. I will give you three days for your answer, and I will have my attorney here when you give me your answer. Three days."

"You're a disgusting despicable human is all I have to say. I will do exactly what I want to and not you, or anyone else, will stop me. I am a strong and independent woman."

She then added, "The police will handcuff you and will lock you up in jail."

"No. The many laws designed to protect women from abusive men also protect men from lawless women. I have spent a great deal of time trying to determine what to do. I am up against a wall and have no choice but to issue an ultimatum. It's totally up to you now."

Bela then screamed "I want you out of my life forever, you horrible foolish man!" She then stormed out of the house, slamming the door and cursing loudly as she left. I was to learn later she went to the sitter's to pick up the kids. "You have three days," I reiterated as she left.

CHAPTER 16
The Crash

After our conversation, I went back to my office to get some work done. Our conversation bothered me, but I felt I had no choice except to do what I did. As I was finishing up some reports, I heard on the six-o'clock news, the following disturbing broadcast:

> A terrible accident occurred today. A late-model Cadillac was traveling at an excessive rate of speed when it barely made the turn onto the viaduct at Twenty-first Street and State Street. Witnesses then described the car as careening toward the guardrail on State Street, and rolling over the guardrail, plummeting hood-first down to the street forty feet below. The car landed head first onto the pavement below. One witness screamed, "Oh, this is horrible, awful, terrible!" There was, seemingly, no way the driver or passenger could have survived the impact. One passerby told the police, "As the car fell, I heard a child frantically scream: 'Help, Daddy! Help, Daddy!' before the car hit the pavement and burst into f lames."

I later learned from the police that the driver, Mrs. Bela Kline, twenty-six, and her two children, Chip and Michael, were all pronounced dead at the scene.

I was stunned. I knew she was out of her mind, high on sex and drugs, but never could I have imagined that she would do something like this. When I told my secretary, Mrs. Willke, she was as stunned as I was.

"I just don't know what to say." She was in tears and gave me a hug. She had been with the company for thirty years: worked for my cousin, my father, and now me. I knew I could not go home, so I just stayed in my office and worked, or tried to.

When I told my mother what happened, she said, "You are going to stay with me for a few days. The news about your family, sadly, was not totally unexpected. Dr. Carter lives next door. I'll ask him to prescribe something to help you sleep."

"I don't think I can drive to your house."

"Then I'll come pick you up. You cannot go to your family home, not yet, maybe never."

Happy, mother's dog who always looked happy, now, at least to me, looked sad. He seemed to read my mind when we arrived home.

Dr. Carter called the pharmacist, who brought the prescription to our home. I plunged into a deep depression that would not lift for many months.

I slept, or tried to, on the La-Z-Boy® chair in the living room. It all seemed so unreal, actually surreal.

The next day, I felt the best thing I could do was go into the office to attempt to keep occupied. Mom drove me there, saying nothing as she drove, except, "I am so sorry. So very sorry. We never expected all this to happen."

The first thing I did was remove all the pictures of my family from my office. I stored them in a drawer in the office storage room and never put them back. Around noon, I was told we had a company meeting in the auditorium.

Because it was not on my calendar, I asked Mrs. Willke what the meeting was about. She always put everything on my calendar, so I was baffled. Mrs. Willke said, "Don't ask questions. Just go." As soon as I entered the auditorium, all our employees stood up and gave me a thunderous applause. I was in tears.

Then the team leader stood up. "We are aware of what has happened and want to say a few words, well, not a few words but a lot of words. We have known you since you were about ten or eleven, and our respect and affection for you has only grown since then."

"I agree," added the head pattern-maker. "You are honest and fair, and this is the best job I have ever had."

Someone then piped in: "This is the only job you have ever had!" That brought some laughter and lots of applause.

At that, Helmut added, "I have worked for four companies in two countries, and there is no doubt this is the best job I have ever had. You are a joy to work for. We are a team. I've always seen you as on our side, helping us in any way you can to do our job." With that, another round of applause burst forth.

"Let me give you an example," the lead lathe operator said. "When I was stuck on meeting the required tolerance specs, you took it upon yourself to bring in a manufacturer's rep to show me what I was doing wrong. He spent a full day working with me. We solved the problem, which was mostly a machine maladjustment issue. It was fixed and now the machine works perfectly."

After several more testimonials, they gave me a sympathy card signed by our almost five-hundred employees. I appreciated the concern immensely, and it did help to take my mind off my loss for an hour or so. I knew then it would be a long time before that hole was filled, if it could ever be.

We had a large funeral for Bela and my children. The only option was a closed casket, but we had a large board with lot of pictures of happier times, pictures I still had a hard time looking at I was afraid I would lose it, so tried to focus on the guests. I noticed a few strange, rough-looking people there that I had never met before. Bela's mother refused to come. Instead, she sent a note on the funeral visitation note blaming her daughter's behavior squarely on me:

> "You put her up to this, you selfish fool. You never did love her, you loved only yourself. You're a horribly evil selfish man!!"

I slowly adjusted to my loss, or tried to. Always an optimist, I felt I could remarry someday and begin again. I dated several women, nice women all of them, but never felt the same thing I felt for Bela in spite of the last few terrible years with her. I missed her and the boys, even if they were technically not mine. I tried to blame the whole problem on myself. I could forgive Bela for everything except killing my children. Especially how she did it was unspeakably cruel.

I was eventually able to move back into my home, the one that Bela and I designed and decorated together. It was hard moving back because in this home were lots of good memories, but I was not there very much anyway. My work was now my life in more ways than one.

I also again began attending church regularly. It gave me a break from work and I enjoyed the association. I also found the sermons very uplifting. I got to know several good people. That helped with the loneliness, but I still missed my family enormously.

At one small group meeting, I approached Christopher about how the Board had found out about Bela's criminal activities.

"I understand that you met with the Board about Bela's criminal record."

"I did, so but found..."

I interrupted, "There's no need to explain. I knew that Bela was in deep trouble. She probably would have ended up dying of a drug overdose or from contaminated street drugs, or murdered as a result of some drug deal gone horribly wrong. Or shot by some of the men she seduced and then she attempted to take to court to extort them with the false claim that they behaved inappropriately toward her sexually."

"I am relieved that you understand my situation as the lead investigator in the drug sting case involving your wife," Christopher replied, with a visible sigh of relief.

"Look, you've always been my best friend, and the incident with Bela does not change that in the least. I found out the Board asked for your input to either dispel the rumors, which was their hope, or to confirm them, which was their fear. They knew that the case would cause the company much harm, and they wanted to prevent any major problems in the future. They also knew that they could trust you."

"I really appreciate your wisdom, Billy," Christopher added to ensure we were still friends.

"I would not be able to respect you if you did anything else. She was a Jezebel. I just refused to accept that fact, even though the evidence was there ever since I first got to know her. I did not want to believe what others clearly saw."

"But Billy, you lost your children, and I feel partly responsible." "Don't. Bela caused the loss of my children purely by her own selfish actions, not you. No one could have predicted what she did. No one." With that we hugged and went our separate ways.

About this time Rebekah called and said:

> "I wanted to give you a call some time, but when I heard about the accident I was stunned by the news. You are a good man and I am sure you were

a very good husband. I have known you since you were a kid and feel horrible about what happened."

"Rebekah, I really appreciate your call. Next to Christopher you are one of my best friends."

"We are more than friends, we are cousins, and don't bother with the details. We are family, period."

We chatted for maybe a half-hour and it really felt good, as always. She was doing great and the news about her warmed me. I needed some good news at times like these.

Later, when at my office, I experienced some groin pain, so made an appointment to see the company doctor. He did some tests then later walked into my office to relay the results to me.

"I found out what the problem is. You have a venereal disease and will need a strong dose of antibiotics, probably penicillin. Are you allergic to penicillin?"

"Not that I know of."

"Good. I will write you a prescription now. Just follow the instructions on the label."

Embarrassed, I explained, "I think I know how I contracted a venereal disease. It was a residue of my wife Bela, I'm sure."

"You do not need to explain to me the cause. My job is to treat the problem. I also found out from the tests we did that you are sterile and cannot have children."

I was stunned! "Is the problem treatable?" I asked, choking on the words.

"Not by any ordinary means, and the commonly claimed treatments may well do more harm than good. You have primary testicular damage from radiation aimed directly at, or near, the testicles. The sperm-forming cells are extremely sensitive to the effects of radiation. Even comparatively low doses can cause irreversible damage to the stem cells in the outer wall of the seminiferous tubules that produce the immature sperm, the spermatogonia."

"What could have caused this? Is it genetic?"

"I checked your medical records and found you had an x-ray for a pelvic injury you sustained when you were running track. It appears that the radiation you received was far too intense."

"And nothing can be done?"

"Nothing I would recommend. One solution is to marry a woman that already has children," he said with a smile, trying to be helpful, help which I had mixed feelings about.

I felt depressed when I learned the news, but would have to heed his advice. I did not want a childless marriage, and knew the number of divorced women with young families was fairly common. But of course I would not marry a woman based on her family. It would be a plus, though. I was busy with other things now, so soon stopped thinking about the question. I did begin to take the antibiotics the doctor prescribed. I knew only one source of the venereal disease was possible.

I also wondered how many other men Bela had infected. I was told later by the company doctor that he contacted the health department to locate persons we suspected were infected by Bela. Then I later learned the number was over twenty-two that we knew of, likely many more. Slightly over half were infected, eleven men. If she only knew how much harm she caused, but she may well have known and was not in the least concerned.

I once ran into Bela's mother while shopping. She walked up to me and, with a look of disgust, spat: "I hope you can live with yourself in view of what you did to my daughter."

"Pardon me? What did I do?"

"A lot. She ran your household and you refused to give her the money she needed to take care of your needs and pay your bills. Time and time again she had to borrow money from me to pay your bills! You drove her to what she did! You selfish miser! You took the checkbook from her and changed the combination of the safe, so she had no choice. To pay your bills she had to borrow money from me. A lot of money, actually. Shame on you, you are a disgusting selfish person!"

I had no idea what to say, so I stood there stunned. I liked her when I first met her, but things had obviously changed drastically since then.

"Then you grossly neglected your own children, and even bugged the house to spy on your own wife! One good thing is your sweet children will never learn what a horrible husband and father you were. That's why she took them with her so they would not have to face what kind of evil man you were."

I only said, "I am sorry, very sorry for what happened," and walked away. From this encounter I learned that Bela had also pressured her mother for money to help pay for her drugs. Stealing from me and earning money from prostitution was not enough. A drug addiction can cost a fortune.

I dated a few women after Bela, but felt guilty because, my self-image told me, I was a married man. Also, as I could not have children, I was at some level attracted to women who already had children, something my mother said was selfish.

"You need to judge a woman solely on the basis of what she is, not on what she has, whether it be money, fame or children," mother once said.

"I know that, mother, but in the back of my mind I see her as a package, just like most women see me as a package. I am not just Billy, but a business man, an entrepreneur."

I was truly disappointed in the few women I had dated, and often felt a little depressed afterward. One problem was I compared every woman I dated to the good qualities in Bela. And she had many good qualities which she manifested during the first few years of our marriage. I actually thought better of her after I lost her. How it ended was a nightmare I'm trying to forget, not very successfully, though. After a while, I felt I needed to be happy as a single man, not a very pleasant thought. It seemed I had to move on, and my life would be my work.

To keep busy I did some volunteering for various church charities. I also was part of a detailed study at my church proving from the Old Testament that Jesus was the promised Messiah. This study was important because it removed a large barrier from my Christian walk.

CHAPTER 17

A Door Opens

O ne day after work I had to pick up a few items from the grocery store. I left early enough to get back home in time to watch the six-o'clock news. I always watched the news to learn about what was going on in the world. It took only ten minutes in the store to get the few things I needed. As I walked out of the store, I noticed a young lady with two young boys in tow, struggling to carry her purchases. All of a sudden, the paper grocery bag filled with her groceries tore open, and the contents spilled on the ground, breaking several glass jars.

"Can I help you with that?" I asked as I walked toward her.

"No, I'm fine," she answered curtly.

"It doesn't look like you are fine to me!" I said, as I began stooping down to pick up the glass shards from the broken jars.

"Let me get a container to put this broken glass into," I mumbled as I walked to my car to retrieve one.

"I always carry recyclable cloth bags as part of my ecology concerns," I said as I walked toward my parked vehicle.

When approaching her family as I returned to help clean up the mess, I overheard her older boy ask, actually complain, "Now what are we going to have for dinner?" With a forlorn look, the mother answered, "I don't know. Money is very tight now."

As soon as I arrived back, I continued to help clean up the mess.

Just then a friend of mine from church, a policeman, drove up. Looking at the woman, as he got out of the police car he asked: "Ma'am, are you all right? Do you need some help?"

When she turned her head toward the cop, he immediately recognized her.

"Oh, hi! You're Roy's widow, Katherine, aren't you?"

"Yes, Phil, I am."

"How are you doing?"

"As well as can be expected, I guess."

"We sure miss your husband at the station. He was a wonderful man and an outstanding officer."

"Thanks. I appreciate the kind words. He sure was that and more. He was a great father, too. His two boys sure miss him."

"Well, Katherine, I see you are in good hands now."

I wasn't sure what he meant by this comment, but she said, "Thanks."

Looking at me, Phil added, "Billy, see you in church on Sunday?"

"Oh, I'll be there," I responded. "I'm on the Pastor Parish Committee and we have a meeting on Sunday."

"That's right. See you on Sunday." With that, Phil got back into his squad car and drove off.

"Do you know him?" Katherine asked.

"Yes, I do," I answered. "We're good friends. We both attend the Baptist Church here in town. Say, I overheard your son concerned about supper. There is an excellent restaurant near this grocery store that we can go to for dinner. I would be honored to treat you and the boys."

"No, we're fine. We'll have something to eat at home."

"It looks to me like you were going to make spaghetti tonight, and it appears to me like that meal is not going to happen."

Just then her oldest boy said, "Oh, mom, can we please go to the restaurant with this nice man?"

Then his younger brother chimed in, adding, "Yes, please

mom? Let's go out to eat. We did not have any lunch and I'm hungry."

After a few more, "Please, mom. Please, mom. Please, mom." pleadings, Katherine agreed. "Okay. I guess I'm outnumbered.

It's three to one, so let's go."

I then thought we needed some formal introductions, so piped up with "Let me formally introduce myself. My name is William Kline, but most of my friends call me Billy. And your name I assume is Kathrine?"

"Yes Kathrine, but I go by Kathy, Kathy Martin."

"I am very pleased to have met you. I am looking forward to dinner!" "We can take my car. The restaurant is only a couple of blocks from here," I said, as I pointed my hand in the direction of my favorite eating place.

"That will work fine," Katherine replied as she flashed a warm smile.

"My car is the black Mercedes right over there, next to that red convertible," I explained, pointing to my car.

I opened my back door so the kids could get in. I still had the car seats in my car, so I buckled both of the boys in. When we were all in my car, I drove the few blocks to the restaurant where I often had lunch with clients. When we arrived, I mentioned "This restaurant has great food but are often very busy at dinner time. So I have some magic tricks in my car to entertain the boys. Magic in my hobby."

So I grabbed my bag of magic tricks and we all went in. The boys were obviously very excited to be eating out.

When we entered the restaurant, I asked for a private dining room. "Right this way, Billy," the maître d'hôtel answered.

We followed her into the private room so the kids could enjoy my entertainment. When in the room, Katherine asked, "How did the waitress know your name? You must come here often."

"I come here several times a week, usually with business associates or customers," I answered.

After we were seated, I asked the two boys their names and ages.

"I am Nathaniel," said the older boy, "I am six years old. Everyone calls me Nathan."

"And my name is Patrick," added the younger boy. "I am four years old. My birthday will be in May!"

As I shook their hands I added "It is great to have met both of you."

"Most people call me Pat," Patrick mentioned as an afterthought. The waitress then arrived and passed out the menus.

"What shall I get you to drink?"

"Kathy?" I asked while looking at her.

"Water is fine for me and the boys." She told the waitress.

"Water is fine for me." I added as I passed out the menus to everyone.

The boys then asked, "Mom, what can we order?" Before she could answer I said, "You boys can order anything you want on the menu. I am paying the bill and I want this to be a special treat! So anything on the menu is yours for the asking."

When the waitress returned for our order, both boys ordered a meal of chicken macaroni and cheese, and added green beans at the insistence of their mother. They obviously really enjoyed eating out and acted as if they had not had a good meal in a while. Kathy then ordered Chicken Fettuccine Alfredo and I ordered the same, a favorite of mine.

The food at this time of day usually requires a twenty minute wait, so while waiting, I did some card and magic tricks to pass the time. The boys were enthralled; most kids are with magic.

I first explained "We call these tricks 'magic' but they are not magic at all, not really. Once you know the trick, anyone can do it. It just takes practice. Often a lot of practice! Have you boys ever been to a magic show?"

"Yes, we had one at our school. It was a lot of fun. I really liked watching it," Nathan answered.

"Do you remember any tricks?"

"Yes. The man at the show at our school did a trick and his wife shot out of a big hat! I was amazed."

"Do you know how he did that?" I asked.

"I have no idea," Nathan answered. It was obvious that Nathan took the lead and his brother Pat usually followed, almost on cue.

"Let me show you," I said, as I took a Jack-in-the-box out of my kit. "How does this work?" I asked.

At that, Pat piped in: "You just turn the crank and up pops the clown!"

"Okay, Pat, show me."

He turned the crank a few times and up popped the clown. They both laughed, as if they'd never seen the box do its magic!

"Let me show you how it works," I said, as I grabbed ahold of the Jack-in-the-box.

"Notice how I can push the head in the box with my hand? The head is on a spring, so when the top is opened it is released and comes out of the box. The wife of your school magician was on a platform and, on cue, she was forced up by the platform just like the Jack-in-the-box, so she appeared to just pop up!"

"Wow," both boys answered in unison.

"It takes a lot of practice, and the contraption to propel her upward has to be well-built so she will be safe. She has to go into the room below the trap door and close the door. When the time is ready, the strong spring pops her out with enough force to push her up! The spring has to be strong enough to get her out, but not too strong. Actually, they probably used a pneumatic system, and not a spring."

"What's a pneumatic system?" Nathan asked, puzzled.

"It's a system that uses compressed air, like a bicycle tire pump."

"Oh, we have one of those to put air in our bicycle tires."

About then the waitress arrived with our order.

After a great meal and an enjoyable evening, I drove them back to their car, a rather beat-up ten-year-old model.

"I had a great time with you and your two boys this evening. Can we do this again?" I asked.

Both boys said, "Yes!" but Katherine said nothing. Instead, she coolly started her car and drove off.

I was disappointed, and felt down all week. I thought she would at least say, "I had a great time, too." She didn't. She didn't say anything. She just drove away.

On Saturday, Phil called and said, "Will I see you tomorrow in church?"

"I don't think so. I haven't been feeling very well lately."

"Well, you are set to receive an award, so take some aspirin, or whatever you need to feel well. Be sure to be there. This Sunday will be an important day for you."

"Okay, I'll try."

"Don't just try, be there! That's an order." He demanded.

"Okay, I got it." Phil doesn't usually order me around like I was a law violator, so I felt I had to go. What was up? What was this award he talked about?

Sunday came and I had to drag myself out of bed and drive to church. "This award better be good," I thought to myself. I really didn't feel like going to church today, not after my let down, which was still bothering me.

CHAPTER 18

A Surprise at Church

I showed up as usual at church and started ushering, one of my responsibilities. We had a good crowd this week because it was a special church growth Sunday event we had to encourage new persons to come. When the service was about to begin, I saw Nathaniel and Patrick running toward me and Katherine following! Both boys gave me a big hug and asked if they could sit by me. I said, "Of course you can!" I had more than one tear in my eyes after I received the hugs. I then led Kathy and the boys over to where I usually sat.

When we were seated, Patrick asked if we could go to that restaurant again for lunch. "Of course we can," I replied, "but only if it's okay with your mother."

"It's fine with me," said Katherine, glowing with a broad smile. "Do you have any more card and magic tricks?" Nathaniel asked.

"Yes, I have a lot more," I said, adding an ear-to-ear grin to my words. After church service ended, the four of us were at my, and now our, favorite restaurant, for lunch.

At the restaurant I asked Katherine how she knew which church I attended. There were, after all, several Baptist churches in town. "From our mutual friend, Phil, of course. He gave me directions and the service times."

We had a great time discussing the events of the week while I showed off my amateur magic trick skills. Actually, the boys were impressed, and that was all that mattered.

Later, I asked about Katherine's coolness when I dropped them off after we had first met.

"I had to be confident that the boys liked you." She explained. We had a long talk about you and their father, and I wanted to know if I could start seeing you. They made the decision. They were ready to explore having another man in the family," she explained. "I've known divorced and widowed women, and the 'new boyfriend' idea can create huge conflicts with the children. They felt their mom was rejecting, or attempting to replace, their biological father. I wanted to avoid that problem, if possible."

She went on, "I also talked to your friend, Phil. When Phil stopped his police car and walked toward us, I first wondered if you were on probation or in some kind of trouble with the law. Then I realized it was Phil. It's been close to two years since I had last seen him. He's a little grayer now, has gained some weight, and has less hair, so I didn't recognize him at first."

"I also asked Phil about you. On my mind were questions like: Were you married? Divorced? Separated? Why did you have car seats in your car? Did you have children? And why did you drive a four door family car?"

To answer these questions, Phil told Katherine a short version of the tragic Bela story. It turned out she remembered what Bela did. The event was all over the papers, and was even on the nightly news.

She first thought my attention to the boys was strange, and was cautious, but soon learned that I was known to be a man who loved children. Kathy felt empathetic, and now could understand why I was so attentive to her kids.

She knew I was good friends with Phil, her husband's former coworker, so knew she could get straight answers to her basic concerns. She could tell I was very attentive to her and was justly cautious. After all, she was a very attractive young women and has had a few bad experiences with men as I had with women. This is why she was so cool after I brought her and the kids back to her car after that first dinner.

She mentioned to Phil that I was just too good to be true! I sure appreciated that comment! I also felt meeting her and her boys was an answer to prayer.

We soon began to spend a lot of time together, the four of us, eating out and enjoying doing things together. Ball games, visits to museums, enjoying movies as a family, and long walks in the park were all on our agenda. I also did some repairs that her house required. Kathy found out I was quite the handyman.

After several wonderful evenings with her and the kids, I asked, "What happened to your husband, Roy?"

"It's a tragic story. He was sitting in his squad car with another policeman, Rudy, his buddy, writing a crime report. An African American man walked up to the car, called my husband a dirty cop, and fired a gun at his left temple, executing him."

"He was murdered?"

"Yes. In response, Rudy opened the right door of the squad car, stepping out far enough to fire several shots at the assailant. It was learned at the autopsy that of the six shots Rudy fired, two hit the assailant, killing him."

"Oh my! Sounds like your husband was the victim of a very straightforward execution to me," I responded, openly showing my surprise.

"He was, but then lawyers for an African American anti-cop organization went to court claiming it was a hate crime. They claimed Rudy did not have to kill the assailant, but was close enough to be able to merely wound him, and by this means stopping him. They claimed he fired six shots out of anger and, if you can believe it, racism! Rudy was an African American, so they argued in court that African American cops can also be racists. A Black who becomes blue, meaning a cop, is no longer Black. To be an African American law enforcement officer is to be part of two communities that are, at times, completely at odds with each other. The case ended up in court."

Amazed, I said the obvious: "Well, if your best buddy was shot for no good reason, what would you do?" I was somewhat surprised at the racist claim, which to me was just a hate cop missive.

"We argued that Rudy knocked his glasses off his face when he stepped out of the squad car to fire at the killer. Because he was very near sighted, he couldn't see as well as he did with his coke bottle glasses on! So, he fired to be sure to hit the man who'd just murdered his best buddy. The jury vindicated Rudy, thank God! Rudy was so upset with the entire ordeal, though, that he resigned from the police department and went to law school. He should graduate next year. He's like the brother I never had."

"I need to add that my husband was never an A-student, but worked hard and had a heart of gold. He never would have made it through the police academy without Rudy. Rudy was from the inner city and, contrary to the stereotype, was sharp as a tack. He started taking college courses on his own as soon as he graduated from high school. He was studying his sociology book one evening when his dad grabbed it away and ripped it up in front of him, literally ripping it into shreds."

"What did you say? Why would his dad do something so stupid?"

His dad explained: "Reading those books ain't never gonna get you anywhere. You gotta learn how to live on the streets, learn how to hustle. You Black and life not fair. You ain't never gonna make it in no white man's world," he declared.

"His father did not do very well in life, but he did take good care of his family, so I do not want to be too hard on him. He just had different values than his son."

"I guess so!"

"Well, Rudy made it through the police academy with flying colors, and my husband would not have graduated if it was not for Rudy's help. They studied together all the time. Police Academy was not easy. They had to do a lot of memory work. They also had to study a lot of science, such as ballistics, fiber evidence, the investigation process, blood analysis, and luminol testing for iron to detect blood residue. Luminol chemiluminescence works well to find evidence of blood even in locations that are wiped clean to the naked eye."

"Sounds complex!" I responded, somewhat lost at the list of topics he had to study.

"I helped him study for his required continuing education hours, so I learned a lot as well," Katherine noted. "Rudy, on the other hand, did not exactly have a football player physique."

"What do you mean by that?" I said, puzzled.

"Rudy was five-feet-ten inches and weighed at the most one-hundred and fifty pounds. Tall and thin, so my husband helped him pass the physical fitness training. They had to run three or four miles in a given amount of time, I forget the number, to graduate from the Academy. Many people never graduate because they cannot meet the high physical requirements required for police work."

"Until now I didn't have a clue about what it takes to be a policeman!" I exclaimed.

"Most people don't. I didn't know much about police work until I married my husband. Then I learned more than I ever wanted to know!"

"So the loss of your husband, Roy, was very traumatic for Rudy."

"They developed a close bond, so close that when one was hired by a police department, he would not take the job unless the other one was also hired. They worked as a team. They stayed that way until my husband was murdered."

Agreeing, I added "It is critical, to say the least, to work as a team in police work. Especially the senseless way he was murdered, just sitting in the squad car writing a police report on a crime. Was the report related to the man who shot him?"

"Not as far as we could tell. The man who shot my husband had no identification on him. We think he was a drug dealer who hated cops. No one claimed the body, so he was buried in an unmarked grave. The state paid the bill."

Katherine and I were married after four short months of courting. We had a large wedding this time in a very different venue. Too many bad memories of Bela. Rebekah was there as well, jokingly explained she did not plan to come to my next wedding! I told her this marriage would last a long time so the next event would be a wedding anniversary. She said, "I'll be there."

"Plan on it!" I responded.

All four of us adjusted very well. We regularly attended my church, and went through counseling to deal with some of our past baggage, which we both had. The critical factor in how well we did was the fact that both Katherine and I could relate to each other due to similar, but very different, traumatic experiences. I was obviously very biased, but thought Katherine was one of the most beautiful women I had ever known. Most importantly, she was beautiful on the inside as well as on the outside.

We also agreed to rear the children in some of the Jewish traditions, including having the coming-of-age ceremony called a bar mitzvah when the boys turned thirteen. We also, in a limited way, celebrated some of the main Jewish holidays, such as Hanukkah. As a few extra presents were involved in this tradition, the boys rendered no objections. After all, Christ was a Jew.

Nathan soon started to shadow me and others at the shop. And about a year later Patrick followed.

I hope they will follow me and someday become the new CEOs of the corporation. I spent as much time with them as I can, helping them pursue their own interests as well. However, they are learning the management role so well, they tell me, that they will someday be running the company . . . perhaps even sooner than I anticipated. They are such a blessing!!

Bela's mom moved back to California and remarried her husband. She told friends there was no reason to stay here anymore, now that Bela and her two grandkids were gone. I had a chance to talk to him once about his ex-wife, now again his wife. "She put me through a nightmare, but I still love her and I always will. We were together since we were freshmen in high school. Love tolerates a lot. As a screenwriter, I know that very well," he added.

He then asked me, "If Bela had not committed suicide and murdered your children would you have divorced her?"

I thought for a moment and answered, "I would have done everything I could to help her straighten her life around, including drug rehabilitation. Divorce was the last thing on my mind. I always loved her, and that never changed in spite of what she did, but I had to protect my children. I was naïve and very frustrated at that time in my life."

"Your children?"

"Yes, in spite of their parentage, I always did, and still do, consider them my children."

"You are a very good man and did what you could to help my daughter. I was honored to have you as my son-in-law. I just wish things turned out differently, but Bela was always a very difficult child. She wanted much more in life than it could ever offer anyone. Fame, money, glamor, excitement, and that drive killed her, as it does so many here in Hollywood. Then she got hooked on drugs."

I wished him happiness and God's blessing, and we parted as friends.

CHAPTER 19

Postscript

F ew people view women as murderers, and historically very few have existed, many involved in crime in conjunction with their boyfriends or husbands. Although fully 99 percent of those on death row in the United States are men, most of the handful of women executed in the United States were truly evil women. Belle Gunness (the name Bela was used in this novel to protect the identity of the woman in the story) was the epitome of a woman who murdered her husband and children for the insurance money. She married very soon after the murders, and her second husband died just eight months later. She again collected a pile of money on the insurance. Between the years 1884 and 1908, Gunness is thought to have killed at least 14 men, perhaps 40 or more in total. Further investigation unearthed the partial remains of at least 11 additional bodies on the Gunness property. The bodies were dismembered and buried in gunny sacks. She found men by using advertisements seeking male companionship, only to murder and rob the men who responded.

She killed most, or all of them, and dismembered their bodies. Ray Lamphere, who was Gunness' hired hand and lover, claimed that Gunness asked him to burn down the farmhouse with her and her children inside. The body thought to be Mrs. Gunness's was likely a murder victim, chosen and planted in the house to mislead investigators. The brother of one victim warned Gunness that he planned to investigate his brother's disappearance. Lamphere claimed that the impending visit of the brother motivated Gunness to destroy her house, fake her own death, and f lee.

Reported "sightings" of Belle Gunness in the Chicago area continued long after she was declared dead. All of these facts are controversial, but what is not is, after Gunness' crimes were publicized, the Gunness farm became a tourist attraction. People came from across the country to see the mass graves. They bought concessions and souvenirs. The crime became an acknowledged part of area history, so much so that the La Porte County Historical Society Museum even has a permanent "Belle Gunness" exhibit.

Some of the minor details of the Bela story were also loosely influenced by Hedda Gabler, written by Norwegian playwright Henrik Ibsen. It becomes clear during the course of the play Hedda had never loved her husband George. She married because she thought her years of youthful abandon were over.

George and Hedda soon became financially overstretched. George tells Hedda that he will not be able to finance the regular entertaining or luxurious housekeeping that she had been expecting. Instead, he has spent the last few years working on what he considers to be his masterpiece, the "sequel" to his recently published work.

Frustrated, Hedda throws the manuscript into the fireplace. Later, leaving the others, she goes into her room and, tragically, shoots herself in the head.

ABOUT THE AUTHOR

D r. Jerry Bergman has worked with inmates in one of the largest walled prisons in America (SPSM; Southern Prison in Southern Michigan; in Jackson, Michigan). He also worked for the Oakland County Probation Department and taught corrections at the college level for several years. In addition, he has developed a college-degree program in corrections and has published widely in this area. He also did research for the National Council on Crime and Delinquency (NCCD) on the criminal population for the community treatment project for second-felony offenders. The results were published by NCCD. His Ph.D. thesis was titled, *Evaluation of an Experimental Program Designed to Reduce Recidivism Among Second Felony Criminal Offenders.* The 886-page dissertation was published in Ann Arbor, Michigan by University Microfilms Publishers. Dr. Bergman also was employed as a therapist at *Arlington Psychological Associates*, Toledo, Ohio, and at the Toledo Pain and Stress Center. This is his 63rd book. So far his books have been translated into 14 languages, most recently in Arabic. There are now over 80,000 copies of his books in print.

Printed in the United States
by Baker & Taylor Publisher Services